ADAM GOLD

Behind Blue Eyes Book 1

SARA J. BERNHARDT

Contents

First Edition

Adam Gold: Behind Blue Eyes, book 1

2018 Lavish Publishing, LLC

All Rights Reserved

Published in the United States by Lavish Publishing, LLC, Midland, TX

Cover Design by: Alexcia Productions

Cover Images: CANSTOCK

Paperback Edition

ISBN: 978-1-944985-69-1

www.LavishPublishing.com

For my Adam

Prologue

MONTAGUE SUMMERS SAID, "Throughout the whole vast shadowy world of ghosts and demons, there is no figure so terrible, no figure so dreaded and abhorred yet did it with such fearful fascination, as the vampire, who is himself neither ghost nor demon yet who partakes the dark natures and possesses the mysterious and terrible qualities of both. Around the vampire have clustered the most somber superstitions, for he is a thing which belongs to no world at all."

I always knew I was different. Even before that fateful day. Even before I moved to Boston. I always felt misplaced. When I was young, I wasn't very good at many things. I loved music, and I wanted to read and to write.

I wanted to engage in conversations about long-ago adventures and wars in faraway lands. My father would tell me, "Get your head out of the clouds, Adam. You need to learn work ethic." My mother was far more understanding and allowed me to go to school even through my father's objections. He was convinced I would not be able to handle it. He was wrong. The first months of school were some of my happiest memories. I adored the routine and organization. Everything was in order, and nothing felt out of place. *I*—didn't feel out of place. For the first time in my life.

It was there I met her—Mary, the beauty with the golden hair and deep gray eyes. It was easy to fall in love with her as I did. She was part of the school choir. I knew I loved her when I first heard her sing, and she returned my affection. We often indulged in inappropriate love making behind the schoolhouse, which fortunately, nobody found out about. She came from a wealthy family and was humble and kind. I was a better man just for knowing her.

It was a year before my wedding when my father fell ill with fever. My mother insisted on caring for him herself. Tragically, the illness took my father and, shortly after, my mother. The doctor said she had caught the same sickness, but I knew it was a broken heart that had afflicted her. Mary had postponed the wedding saying it was "too soon."

After my father's death, and the fortune and estate he left to me, I saw no reason to wait any longer. I wanted to start a life for myself, and I needed my wife to do it.

It was April of 1792 when Mary and I were blessed with a beautiful baby girl, Madeline. The day she was born, she didn't even cry, just cooed and gazed around with her eyes wide open. Even as an infant, her eyes were a soft green as they had been in her childhood and her hair golden like her mother's.

We lived in my beautiful home in Switzerland for five

years until 1797 when French general Napoleon Bona-parte, who had just successfully conquered Northern Italy, sent French military to the city of Geneva. We knew it was time to find a safer home for our family.

I didn't want to leave home, but I knew I had no choice. After an evening outing, Mary had proposed we move to America.

She stared motionlessly into my blue eyes, standing very still with her hands clasped together in front of her, pressing wrinkles into her yellow dress. I saw the look in her eyes and her flaxen hair piled upon her head in lovely curls. She was too beautiful. I tried to look at anything but her, for I knew what she was thinking and feared I could not refuse her. I locked my gaze on the cabinet of finely painted china to her left or the oil lamp on the table to her right. I even stared at the floor, studying the patterns and colors in the rug. I loved her and knew I could not deny her anything. I sighed and continued to look around at all our lovely, fancy things. I took my hat off and hung it on the rack before turning back to face her. The light was dim and cast a lovely glow upon her face, and when at last I looked at her, I knew I could do nothing more. I began to speak then paused, and urging the words from my mouth, I asked, "Where to?"

She didn't hesitate a response. "Boston!" she yelled. "Boston!"

"Why, darling, do you wish to be so far away?" I asked her, hoping I could somehow change her mind.

"With your father's money, we can live anywhere we wish, and Geneva has been our home for so long. I dream of getting out, Adam. I dream of seeing other places. And Boston… Oh, it sounds wonderful, doesn't it?" She lightly bounced in excitement with a wide smile on her perfect face.

I knew I could not deny her anything. She took a step forward, and I brushed my hand across her cheek. I pulled the pin from her piled hair and watched as it fell loose over her shoulders. "Yes," I answered. "Yes, of course it does."

"Boston," she repeated in a whisper. "That is where I wish to go."

I had to do something, didn't I? I had to try something. I took her hands in mine and looked into her eyes, asking my mind for some words of protest. I noticed the way she was looking at me. She was admiring me like she did when we were very young, almost reading through me. I could say nothing besides exactly what I was feeling when she stared at me that way.

"I love you," I whispered.

She smiled. "Does this mean you agree?"

I swallowed, trying again to think of something else I could say. I couldn't tell her how much I detested the idea. "Boston it is."

Chapter One

WE WERE able to book passage on a cargo ship leaving for America the next week. Lake Geneva would take us to the vast North Atlantic. The ship was grand, with large white sails and a swiss flag billowing from the bow. It wasn't free of rats, but the weather had been blessedly calm. Little Madeline was silent as we boarded. Her eyes were wide with anxiety and confusion.

"Where are we going, Papa?" she asked, clinging to my legs.

"I told you, to Boston, where we will live." I ran my fingers through her curls to try and calm her fears.

My heart was heavy, and by the eighth day at sea, I already missed Switzerland. I spent the following weeks a silent, sorrowed man. I stood on the deck, watching the water below me. It was dusk, and I stared at the reflection of the sunset in the waves.

"Adam?"

I turned to see Mary. "Yes, darling?" I replied, pushing the sorrow from my voice.

"Are you all right, my love?"

"I am," I replied. "I am just anxious to arrive is all."

She smiled. "Aye. I am anxious as well. Only a while longer."

I tried to smile but wasn't sure if I had. I still couldn't tell her how unhappy I was with our plans. Aside from my homesickness, something else felt amiss. I had a very uneasy feeling.

The following night as I was trying to sleep, that feeling came again, stronger this time. My stomach was in knots, and my ears were burning as if I were coming down with fever. I got up from the bed, deciding the cold air may help. I stood out upon the deck, but the sensations only became stronger. I truly began to believe something terrible was about to happen, something ghastly aboard this ship, hiding in the shadows. I tried to shake off the paranoia, attempting to convince myself it was nothing, and headed back to the room.

I stepped into the room, and Mary rushed into my arms in hysterics. Sobs tore from her chest. I could feel the convulsions as she clung to me.

"Adam..."

"Mary, what is it?"

For a moment, she continued to weep uncontrollably. "Madeline," she choked out between sobs.

I pushed her gently aside and reached for the oil lamp. I stumbled as the ship began to rock heavily, and I felt the skin on the bottom of my foot tear open from a cracked floorboard. I gasped and tried to ignore the wet feeling of the blood I was spreading across the floor.

"Mary!" I called again, grasping her by her delicate shoulders until she at last calmed her weeping.

She stared at me with red, frightened eyes.

"What's wrong with Madeline?" Terror spread through me like a plague, and my heart rate quickened. I knew then my senses were right. I believed God himself had been trying to warn me.

"Look at her, love," Mary choked. "Look at her."

As I gazed into my daughter's eyes, all my senses seemed heightened. I could feel the rocking of the ship, which had calmed and become gentle. I could feel the love of Mary flowing through my blood simply by the joining of our hands. I could feel her tears soaking into me, coursing through me.

Dark circles surrounded the sunken in green eyes of my once beautiful daughter. It was not that porcelain doll of a child I once knew but the ghost of that same child, barely clinging to life. Her breathing was labored. She was sweating madly yet shivering. Her once perfect skin was encased in a horrible, red rash.

"I'm here, baby girl." I fought desperately to hold back my own tears. I held her hand and looked to Mary, who had still not stopped weeping.

"Call the doctor," I said.

She nodded and headed out of the room to find the ship's medic. She came back moments later with whom I could only assume was the doctor.

"What seems to be the problem?" he asked, opening his bag of supplies.

"She's very ill," I said.

The doctor knelt beside the bed, staring into my child's eyes. He lifted her gown to determine what had caused the rash. "Hmm."

"What is it?" Mary asked. I could hear the apprehension in her words, for we were both terrified of the answer.

"I'm sorry to inform you that your daughter is afflicted with Scarlet Fever," he said. "Keep her head cool. I'm afraid there isn't much else that can be done. I suggest you pray, sir. It is in God's hands now."

Mary stared at me, as if begging me to do something. I didn't know what to say, so I did what the doctor said, and I prayed. I prayed hard through most of the night.

The next morning, I awoke after a very restless sleep and saw that Madeline's eyes were open, but I could still hear her almost gasping for breath.

"Mama?" she whispered.

Mary awoke immediately, if she had been sleeping at all. "I'm here, Madi," she said. "Everything is going to be all right. I'm going to get you some water. Just rest."

She stood from the bed and pulled on a cloak. I placed my hand on her shoulder, and she turned to look at me.

"She'll be all right," she said, even as the tears stained her cheeks. "She just needs some water, and she'll be all right."

I didn't reply. She stared into my eyes for a moment before falling against my chest in tears once again.

The day dragged on slower than usual. By mid-morning, after watching my child's life fading away, I began to lose control. I tried to hold it back but to no avail. I rushed to the edge of the ship, crying out to God.

"Have mercy!" I cried out. "Avere pietà!"

The true realization of death crashed into me and shot through me like a javelin, forcing my body to heave uncontrollably. I had no power here. There was nothing I could do but watch my daugher die. We fled from our home for a better life, and now tragedy struck us like a curse. There was no justice. I cried out to God, cursing his name, but I could not stand that he did not curse me back. The empty air and pain stuck me, breaking me down to the same despair Madeline was feeling. I fell to my knees, screaming to the wind, over the roaring of the ocean.

"Adam!" I heard.

I ignored, consumed by my despair.

"Adam, stop."

I felt Mary grasp my arm, trying to pull me to my feet.

"Please," she pleaded. "Calm yourself."

How frightened she must have been to feel me struggle from her tender touch, as I had never done. I flailed as if trying to escape. I felt my arm collide with her chest, sending her crashing to the floor.

"Adam!" she screamed again, this time half weeping between breaths.

Only moments later, she was holding me down again, pinning my arms to my sides, and kissing me, trying so hard to relax me.

At last my breathing eased. I looked into her gray eyes and wrapped my arms around her, weeping hysterically in the comfort of her warmth.

"Madeline," I whispered. "Oh, God—have mercy!"

I looked to the edge of the ship and thought of jumping into the green waters. I thought of preparing myself for the pain it would cause me, but even as I thought this, I knew I never intended on doing it.

I felt lost, as if I couldn't breathe, and I lay on the

floor with my eyes closed. I could feel my heart in my head, and my eyes filled with new tears after the old had finally ceased. For hours it seemed, I lay there on the floor, staring at the heavens until finally I was calm. We retreated to our room to be with Madeline.

It was fear that awoke me. I opened my eyes, realizing it was dark outside, and I could hardly make out the face of my child, but I could tell she was sleeping, as was Mary. Both were sound asleep in the bed. If only I could speak to them now, to let them know I was well and to tell them of things to comfort my mind from the silence, mostly just to tell them how much I loved them, but I couldn't bring myself to wake them.

When I gazed at my daughter's face and angelic eyes shadowed by her thick, golden curls, I knew I wanted to live no longer. I felt myself sinking back into that same nothingness as I had before; I tried to keep myself from crying out as those thoughts of emptiness all rushed back to me, crowding my mind.

Chapter Two

I GOT up from the warm sheets of my bed and walked out upon the deck, listening to the rushing waters beneath me. I closed my eyes for a moment and opened them to see only black. I wanted to gaze upon the same blue and green Atlantic as I had before, but the waters of night were always black. I sighed, staring out into the darkness, wishing I could just disappear into it. *Become* the darkness. I was lost in the dreams for a moment until I was pulled almost violently out of my thoughts by a voice. I could hear it as clear as day, yet it seemed to be coming from another place—a place far away. It said my name, but I turned to see nothing but the misty deck.

Adam.

I spun on my heels, breaking away from the edge of the ship, searching for the source of the voice. It was deep, dark, and round. It was ghostly and almost inhuman.

"Hello?" I called out.

I turned around again to fight, or perhaps flee, but

there was no one there. The voice laughed mockingly and whispered my name again. I gasped, backing away, but there was nowhere to go, no place to hide. The feelings of evil came rushing back to me. I felt a sense of future pain, a strong foreboding of something truly vile. As if created by the shadows, a figure appeared before me. He moved almost like mist, moving toward me. I backed up, back toward the edge of the ship. He advanced, closing the space between us. As he came closer, I could see he was young, but something about him seemed amiss. His eyes were a tense and dark amber that almost appeared to be glowing. They were deep as if a story of a thousand pages could be read within them.

"Who are you?" I demanded.

His eyes narrowed beneath his golden eyebrows. The voice laughed, yet the man's lips did not move. He stepped closer, and I broke into a panicked sprint. I was unaware where I was going, but I couldn't stop. I ran until my blood felt cold through my limbs. I fled until my lungs burned, and then I knew I had to stop somewhere. I raced below deck and into the storage unit. I moved slowly, finding a place to keep hidden. I stopped behind a stack of crates and hit my elbow on the corner of a wine rack, causing it to tremble.

I could still hear his laughter ringing in my head.

"Leave me, you devil," I cried out.

I crawled behind more of the cargo marked for America. I sat with my knees drawn up to my chin to catch my breath. It was blessedly quiet, and I let out a long sigh of relief. My voice erupted into a scream when I felt the brush of flesh upon my cheek. Before I could flee, I was held captive in strong, unyielding arms. That same rush of terror consumed me once again. I wanted to call for help, but my voice was caught in my throat. I could feel myself being pulled from the ground, my feet hovering. I must have been mad. I saw the deck at least seven feet below me. Wasn't it just moments ago that I was hiding *below* deck?

I struggled in his grasp, but he effortlessly gripped even tighter to my pale arms. I could feel his heartbeat, like the beating of a drum. I knew his body as if it were my own. I felt his life in his flesh. His white complexion and fierce eyes. He truly looked like an angel, but my senses did not tell me he was there to help me. My muscles relaxed, and I gave up the struggle. He had the strength of twenty men, and there seemed no sense in fighting. Wasn't it a short while ago I was telling myself I wanted to die?

As I contemplated, I prepared myself for agony—for an excruciating death. My name came again, slowly, in a sort of whisper but clear as if it were coming from inside my own head. I squeezed my eyes shut in anticipation for something horrific. There was no pain at first, just a warm, almost tender pressure against my throat. Then it came—the sharp, burning feeling in my flesh. My eyes sprang open in shock, but I was unable to scream. I opened my mouth, but nothing came out.

A rush of stories and childhood terrors came rushing back to me, but I pushed the words away into the deepest tunnels of my mind. I could not bare to think on them. I felt no more evil as I was slowly lowered to the ground. Or perhaps I did feel evil, but it did not vex me any longer.

I awoke as if from a nightmare. I realized I was still

outside upon the deck. The first thing my eyes met was that white face and those cat-like eyes sinking into me, burning through me. I tried to speak, but my muscles tightened and tensed, stripping my breath from my lungs. I knew then that I was dying—and there was no one there to save me. My heart was on fire like I was being burned alive from the inside out. I tried to scream, but only a groan escaped.

"I know what you need," the stranger said. "I can give it to you."

I knew in that moment I did not truly wish to die. I feared it more than anything. I feared the uncertainty, the unanswered questions. The agony was unbearable, but I wanted to live.

I tried with all the strength I could muster to speak. "Help me. Please."

The words were barely audible, but he seemed to have heard me.

"You know what you need, my friend. Tell me you want it."

He stared into my eyes again, and I heard his voice in my head. I refused to believe what he was telling me. It couldn't be possible; it couldn't be—true. He whispered one word.

Blood.

Hoping with everything within me that he could save me from the unbearable, unwavering suffering, I spoke again, telling him simply what I thought he wanted to hear—anything to stop the pain. "Yes," I choked. "I want it."

He slowly lifted his wrist toward his open mouth and bit down aggressively. He loomed over me, dripping the hot liquid upon my lips. I tried to resist, but as the blood seeped into my mouth, my body relaxed and the pain dissipated, leaving nothing but pleasure and peace. It was all I ever needed. It was *everything*.

I could hear his heartbeat accelerating until it was beating in perfect unison with my own. I reached up, grabbing his wrist and widening the wound with my teeth, hungry for more, hungry as if it could never be satiated. I never wanted it to end, but he pulled away from my grip. Passion, love, and trust came thrusting into me, and I tried to yell out to him. I tried telling him of this love, but I could not—as the pain came back, searing and scorching me. I felt as if my insides were being ripped from my body, torn out of me without mercy.

"Don't struggle," the stranger said. "Your human body is being cleansed, letting you pass through. Don't fight it."

I writhed on the floor of the deck, trying to do as he said—trying to let the pain take me where it needed to. I waited—waited for the pain to cease, waited for the euphoria to return.

Slowly, it happened. My breathing ceased completely, and my body became soft—as if I were encased in velvet.

"Look around," the man said.

I stood and gazed round. The night didn't appear so dark now. Everything was clear and crisp even in the distance. If there were one in front of me, I would have been able to follow the flapping of a hummingbird's wings.

Anxiety soon crept in, and I gasped, backing into a stack of crates.

The creature laughed. "Don't be frightened."

"Wha—what…?"

"I have given you what you desired."

"What do you know about my desires?" I peeved.

"More than you can imagine," he answered. His voice rang in my ears even though his lips hadn't moved. "What I have given you, Adam—is freedom."

Everything felt different. My body and my mind felt renewed, changed. I couldn't comprehend what he could have done to me. Who was this man? If a man, he was at all.

I brought my eyes back to his. "Freedom?"

He smiled, revealing pointed canines. "Freedom," he echoed. "I am free in ways you could have never known before now. Free in ways you never could have imagined without me."

"I don't understand," I started, taking notice that even my voice sounded different. It rang with a dark, round, and deep tone. "What have you done to me?"

"You know what I have done to you," he said. "Those words that came to your mind, Adam. Do you think they came from nowhere?"

"What words?"

"The ones you were trying not to think. The ones you tucked away in the recess of your mind, hidden away."

My breath caught in my throat, but I managed a whisper. "Vampire."

He smiled like a proud teacher.

I lost my breath completely and sank to my knees.

"Stand up," he demanded.

"It's not possible," I said, getting back on my feet. "It can't be. You must be mad."

"Mad?" He laughed. "Is that what you are truly feeling? Is what you see and what you felt nothing but a fantasy?"

"It must be." I approached him, staring into his glowing eyes. "Tell me, you wicked beast. Tell me what you have done to me."

He threw his head back laughing and placed a hand on my chest, pushing me away. "You make me laugh, Adam Gold."

"Yes, and how do you know my name?"

He stepped very close—too close—and stared into my eyes. "I told you more than you even realize yet."

Again, his lips hadn't moved, and I found myself once again pressed against the crates.

My thoughts raced and swam through my brain. Maybe he was not mad. Perhaps it was I who was mad. Perhaps this creature didn't even exist. I closed my eyes and took a deep breath, which seemed completely unnecessary. When I opened my eyes, nothing had changed.

"My name," the vampire started, formally bowing like a nobleman, "Victor Miller."

I smiled at him, intrigued, and his face grew soft for a moment. He reached into the inside pocket of his heavy, black jacket and revealed a hand mirror. He handed it to me, brushing back the long strands of golden hair from his eyes.

"Many believe our kind do not have reflections," he said. "Clearly, you can see that is a misconception."

I gazed into the mirror, and my heart plunged into my stomach. I looked just as he did. My skin was white and smooth like porcelain, my eyes fierce and illuminated like the eyes of a wolf. My canine teeth were elongated and sharp. There was almost no color in my cheeks or lips. I stared into that mirror for a long time, searching for a single trace of my humanity, a single line or shadow of the old Adam. I found comfort only in the purity of my blue eyes. "What am I?"

"Stop asking those questions," Victor said. "I have given you everything. A life without pain, a life without fear or death. Freedom, Adam. I have given you freedom. Remember—drink from me and live forever."

"Forever?"

"Forever. Sickness and death mean nothing to you now."

None of it made sense to me but nor could I ignore the sensations I had experienced. They were feelings no human could know.

It was a difficult and frightening thing to understand —that I was no longer human. Now I could not die, could not fall ill. I was safe in the power of my new existence. I thought for a brief moment I may have been dreaming, but I couldn't wake up. I remembered Victor's words.

He said something about being cleansed—being rid of my human assets.

I felt as if the blood in my veins had thickened, and my mind focused on nothing else…nothing but blood. I had to believe him. Nothing else made sense. I knew now how I must thrive, how he thrived—feeding off the blood of the living.

He turned to leave, but I stopped him.

"Wait!" I cried. "Don't go. What am I supposed to do?"

"Relax," he answered. "You know what to do."

"No. You can't leave me. I cannot do this without you."

He huffed and turned away. "If you wish to leave the humans in peace, you may have no other choice than to feed off the rats that infest this place. Trust me, Adam. Look into your mind. You know how to kill. I have released that knowledge and that power into you through my gifted blood." He sighed again and looked at me.

He placed a cold hand on my shoulder. "It will be dawn soon. Be here tomorrow evening. Just keep away from the sunlight!"

"If I come here tomorrow…?"

"Yes," he replied. "I'll be here. Keep. Away. From. The sun!"

I nodded, still feeling the surreal haze of uncertainty.

Chapter Three

IT WAS ALMOST dawn when I returned. I crawled into bed, feeling as if I hadn't slept in days. Mary was understandably distressed.

"Are you all right, my love?" she asked.

"I am," I replied. "Only tired. The sorrow has tired me. I need to rest is all."

"Aye," she answered softly. "I shall let you rest."

Mary woke me later that day but thankfully did not open the curtains. Victor told me to stay away from the light.

Mary crawled into bed beside me. She began speaking to me the way she used to years ago. She spoke of undying love and unconditional loyalty. She began kissing me, but I didn't respond. Her breathing became heavy as she moved her lips across my neck and down to my chest. I wasn't enjoying it. I wanted to reciprocate; I wanted to feel. But alas, I couldn't have cared less.

"What's the matter with you?" she demanded.

"I am fine. Just tired."

I didn't want to make love. I had no interest. I knew why, of course. Victor was to blame. I was no longer human. He had taken away all my human qualities. How could I tell her this? How could I tell her that I *couldn't* make love anymore? How could I make her understand? I never wanted to hurt her, but I knew I had. Maybe I really was mad after all.

I didn't know how long I slept, but when I awoke, it was growing dark. I saw Madeline was awake as well. I kissed her cheek and left to wait on the deck.

"You're early," I heard.

I jumped back, feeling foolish when I realized it was only Victor.

He laughed.

"What's so amusing?" I asked.

"Just you," he said, still smiling. "You're still so…"

"So…what?"

"Human," he said. "You're still so human."

"Is that a bad thing?"

"It will not serve you well to hold on to it, Adam. It will only cause you pain and regret."

"Maybe I want those things. Maybe I want to be human."

"But you aren't," he argued. "That is what you haven't yet come to fully understand. You are not human, and you never will be again. You will never grow old, you will never get ill, and you will never die."

"But I feel pain now," I said. "Inside."

"You're hungry. That's what it feels like. That dry ache—now you know."

"So, what am I to do?"

"I told you. It's best to not draw attention to yourself, as there is no way off this ship. Feed on the rats."

"We can live that way?"

He shrugged. "It's not ideal. It's only a means of survival. It will not strengthen you, and it may not even satisfy you, but it will dull the pain."

"So, I don't need to kill?"

"You'll get used to killing. I've told you this, Adam. It is in our nature to destroy. We are a predatory species. The sooner you accept that, the better off you will be. You are free now. Free from old age, sickness, and death."

"What about the sunlight?"

"Ah, yes. The sun and fire. The burning of your remains is the only thing that can kill you."

"So, we are mortal in a sense...?"

"If you would like to call it that—yes."

"If we do not need human blood—"

"Don't," he interrupted. "It doesn't matter. Even if you do not want to feed off mortal blood, you won't be able to resist it."

"What?"

"We are predators, Adam. That doesn't change because you wish for it."

"So—I *have* to kill?"

"And even if you don't have to—you will."

Anger brewed within me turning to rage. "You turned me into a monster!" I screamed. "A murderer!"

"I gave you what you asked for."

"Asked for? I never asked for this."

"Yes," he answered, stepping closer to me. "You did

ask for this. You asked for a way to save your daughter. She's dying, isn't she?"

"How do you know about that?"

"I know what's inside you. I can read your thoughts. Come now—you can do it too."

"Read your thoughts?"

"Not mine. I have put up a barrier in my mind. A dam to hold back the tide. You will learn to do the same in time."

I sighed. "Yes. Madeline is dying."

"You can save her now."

"What?" The realization of what he was asking of me clicked in my mind. "Not like this. I never asked for *this*."

"You wanted a way to save her."

"I can't, Victor. I cannot do that to her."

"Adam, you can. There is no evil in it. What does she deserve? To die? Or to be blessed with eternal life, free from the pain she is suffering now?"

I shook my head mechanically.

"You need to learn," he continued. "If you want her—take her."

I did want her. That, I could not deny. Of course I did. She was my daughter, my child. Shouldn't I, as her father, save her if I had the power to? I watched as the waters beneath me roared, and I thought of death. I thought of Madeline. It was making me sick to think about her imminent death. I had that nagging worry twisting my stomach into knots. If I let her die, would that be the same as killing her? I knew I could never forgive myself if I were to let her die. Not when I had the power to save her. Curse or no curse, I knew what I had to do.

Victor shattered my thoughts.

"I must say," he started. "This ship takes less time than anticipated. By the time we reach the shore, you will be without me."

"Without you? How can I be without you? I need you."

"You don't need me. You can do this on your own. I won't be far. I will be watching out for you always. I promise."

"But I do not want you to leave me. I—"

"Don't say it, Adam," he said, raising his voice. He stepped forward, pointing a finger at my chest. "Do not say you love me. There may come a time when you feel hatred toward me for what you are. There may come a time when you wish me dead. Do not say you love me."

"I don't understand. You said this is what I wanted, what I needed."

"Yes, but that doesn't mean you won't have questions—questions that cannot be answered. It doesn't mean you won't have times when you feel you cannot cope with immortality—when there is too much time left in your life. Who will you blame then?"

"That doesn't change how I feel."

He turned away. "But I do not wish to hear it."

I said it to myself. I couldn't help it. I did love him—I *do* love him. I knew he could read my thoughts, but I didn't care.

He turned back to face me.

"I don't want to do this alone," I said. "I want you to teach me. You say you released all this knowledge through your blood, but...it cannot be so. I still feel so..."

"Lost?"

"Yes."

He placed a hand on my shoulder and leaned forward, looking intently into my eyes. "That's all right. You think I never feel lost? Confused? I do, Adam. We all do. This existence is imperfect, but unlike the human condition, we are free. We can choose to embrace that loss and that confusion and just be."

"Be what?"

"What we are. Just exactly what we are."

"I want to be good," I said. "I want to be virtuous. I want to be a man of God."

"Do not turn to God for answers. When you are unstable, find one who can hold you."

I didn't reply.

"You may have heard many things about what people call 'the undead.' Many fictitious stories and narratives. Very few are accurate."

"Like the mirror."

"Yes."

"You said undead?"

"We are not truly alive, Adam. Therefore, we cannot die. We're not human. Do not be alarmed when blood falls from your eyes when you weep."

"What?"

"You gave up your human biology. It's all only blood now."

I pressed my fingers to my temples. "I'm dead?"

"You are undead," Victor argued. "Immortal. We are somewhere between the living and the dead. I must leave now. I will be near. I promise."

He turned to leave again, but this time, I did not stop him.

I wasn't yet ready to speak with Mary. I didn't know what I was supposed to say to her. But I would not delay my task. If I did not save Madi now, it may have been too late. I had to return. I walked slowly, trying to find my bearings. I couldn't fall apart now. This was crucial.

I heard voices behind me, and I halted, whirling around toward the sound. There was nothing. I could see mortals in the distance. I could see them moving boxes and crates. Their lips were not moving, but I heard their voices. I could hear...their thoughts—their fears, their dreams, their desires. I tried to block it out, push it away, but it wasn't working. The voices began mingling, being drowned out by others. There were so many of them that they all blurred together in deafening noise. I cried out, dropping to my knees, covering my ears with my hands as if it could stop the clamor. I felt a hand on my shoulder, and I screamed, reaching for the stranger, intent on tearing them to shreds as the fear swallowed me whole.

"Adam, it's all right."

I saw I had my hands gripped firmly around Victor's throat. He pulled away. My eyes were still as wide as saucers, and the voices hadn't stopped.

"It's okay," he said. I could barely hear him over the racket, but he was calm.

"Make it stop!" I cried. "Please, make it stop!"

"Shh. Adam, focus. Concentrate on my voice."

I listened as hard as I could, only to Victor, to the wind, to the waves. I listened to everything but the voices until at last they quieted. They faded into the background as faint whispers on the wind.

"See?" Victor soothed. "You don't have to listen."

"You're still here."

"Of course I am. I told you I will always be near."

"I never want to hear them, Victor. Any of them —ever."

He nodded. "I understand. It's frightening."

"It feels wrong like…"

"An invasion?"

"Yes."

He offered me his hand and lifted me to my feet. "It's all right now. Just focus on other things, and the voices will stop."

"Thank you."

"Go to your child now."

Through the crisis, I had almost forgotten about Madeline. "Yes. Of course."

I left to my room and stared at the corpse-like face of my darling daughter. Even in her condition, her green eyes glistened beautifully. I glanced at Mary to make sure she was sleeping.

"Listen to me, Madi," I whispered, brushing the curls from her face. "I'm going to give you a gift, all right? I'm going to give you some medicine so you will be in no more pain."

I thought she may have tried to smile, but it was weak, no more than the shadow of an attempt. The rushing of her blood suddenly filled my ears, and again, I pressed my hands against them to stop the sound. The thumping of her heart was an assault on my senses, and I knew then—the thirst wanted her. The dry, aching pain in my body needed to be relieved. I leaned in toward her and bit into the soft flesh of her neck. Her blood flowed quickly and filled me with an ecstasy I could not describe. The blood was thick and hot. It rolled through me like liquid fire. I could feel the life being drained out of my child, her heartbeat dying down. She was dying. I was killing her—and I couldn't stop. I knew her then. I knew everything. As her blood flowed through me, with it came her thoughts, her secrets, her pain, and her joy. Everything she was was released into me.

I tried to pull away. I tried with everything I had. This was Madeline—my Madeline. This was my child, my purpose, and my everything. I pulled back, almost grieving at the ending of the feed. I stopped for a moment, savoring the pleasure and begging myself to relax. I knew then Victor was right. I would not be able to resist killing. The remorse overcame me, but I could not think on it now. Madeline was still alive.

I bit into my wrist as Victor had done for me and pressed it to Madi's lips.

"Drink," I said frantically. "It's going to be all right."

I knew she was no longer conscious, so I spoke to her mind as my blood dripped into her mouth. Her eyes sprang open, and she gripped my arm in her delicate, little hands and sucked furiously at the wound.

I felt that dry ache return. I felt as if she had broken the very circuit of my life. I pulled back with all my strength, falling to the floor, gripping my chest in agony.

I don't know exactly what went on while I lay on that

floor, half drained of my life. I begged my mind to wake up, but I lay unconscious upon the wooden ground. The blood tears lay in my eyes. I felt a new sense of power now. As my strength slowly returned, I heard my daughter's breathing. It was no longer shallow and labored. I sat upright, gazing at her. She was sitting up in bed, smiling at me. I was powerful. I was strong. Me—the beautiful, arrogant man I had always been. I was more than that now. I was capable of anything, and I had shared this with my baby.

I watched as her eyes gathered the light, glowing in the darkness. She was strong; I could feel it. I could feel a kind of potency emanating from her. Her fever had vanished, and her skin was clear and smooth like my own. She looked once again like the child I knew, only more beautiful than she had ever been.

"Where is Mama?" she whispered.

I had almost forgotten about Mary. Of course, I had to take her too so we could all be together forever.

"Mama is right here, darling. Give me just a moment." I kissed Madi's cheek and moved toward my sleeping wife. Before my teeth pricked her neck, a strange presence scattered my thoughts. An odd force pounded in my brain and through my shoulders to the souls of my feet. There was a strong tremor in the atmosphere, a rush of random notes, like badly played music. Confusion came over me. A cold death came over my face. I could feel the blood rushing to my cheeks. Somehow, I knew. I knew it was an immortal, but my senses told me also that it was not Victor. Impossible. Could there really be another vampire aboard this ship?

There must have been. I could feel the very essence of his life.

I gazed through the darkness and pried my focus into his thoughts. I was given one clue—hair the color of smoke. My mind searched for more, but there was nothing.

I heard Madeline whisper, "Mama."

I rushed to Mary's side. "Mary," I whispered. She didn't stir. "Mary, darling, wake up." She still did not rise. I started lightly shaking her but to no avail.

"Mama?" I heard Madeline again. I could tell she was fighting tears.

"Mary!" I cried out.

I couldn't hear her heart. I couldn't hear the pumping of her blood, and when I pushed myself into her thoughts, I saw nothing. I knew then the one thing I did not want to accept. I threw myself over her body, letting out a wail of terror and despair. Her body was still warm, but I knew she was dead. Her neck was broken, and blood pooled out from deep puncture wounds in her throat. I knew she was gone. I waited too long. I was too late.

"Papa!" Madeline screamed. "Papaaa!"

I wrapped her in an embrace and hushed her. With her voice, she could shatter all the glass on the ship. I cradled her in my arms like I did when she was a baby and we fell apart, sobbing hysterically, unable to stop.

I do not know how long we sat there together wallowing in our grief, but I was finally unable to cry any longer.

"Madi, darling, everything will be all right," I said. "We will avenge this evil. I promise you."

I couldn't even think yet about what I could do to stop

this—to fix it. Mary had been murdered, but we had to keep it a secret. There was no way we could let anyone on the ship know about this. It could expose us to those who would wish us harm.

"You have to try and stay quiet, Madi," I whispered. I could hear the sorrow in my voice, but I tried my best to hide it. "Everything will be all right."

I moved away from her and saw that her silken nightdress was drenched in blood, as was my shirt. I was horrified for a moment until it occurred to me.

"Look, Madi," I started. "You cry blood. There is no horror in it."

She gazed at her nightgown and started tearing at the fabric with her hands, whimpering and gasping.

"It's all right. It's all right. It's just tears, Madi, nothing more."

"Tears?"

I nodded. "You're all right. Don't be afraid. Everything is fine now."

Her eyes still held a look of fear and confusion.

"You'll get used to it," I told her. "I promise."

She stared at me for a moment then nodded.

"I'm going to get us some fresh clothes."

After changing, I helped Madeline out of her stained nightdress. I draped one of my linen shirts over her shoulders and buttoned it quickly, eager to get the stained garments out of my sight. I washed the caked blood off our faces and dropped the clothing overboard, thinking as I did so that if they were to be found by a mortal, they would simply assume sharks were to blame.

Before sunrise, I wrapped Mary's body in a bedsheet and gently pushed her into the dark waters. Madi and I wept then but tried to keep the blood from soaking our clothing again. Everything seemed so unfair. I was given this dark blood to save my child, but now I had lost my wife, and Madeline had lost her mother. How was I going to teach her to live without her? How could I possibly be enough?

Chapter Four

THE SHIP blessedly docked after dusk, and Madeline and I grabbed our luggage and headed to the shore. The mortals were busy hauling crates and boxes off the ship, but I still worried we may attract attention. Our white, smooth, poreless skin was nothing like the colors in human flesh. We walked slowly, hand in hand. I glanced up now and again, making sure no one was looking at us or noticing Mary was not with us.

I scanned my surroundings, searching for Victor. He was nowhere to be seen. I sighed to myself.

It was strange that the suitcase in my hand felt so weightless, almost as if it were empty. Madeline didn't seem to be struggling with hers either. She hadn't even asked me to carry it for her. There were still so many things I was yet to discover about my new existence.

We walked down the streets, but I decided it would be best to get a hotel room for the day before we headed to the manor I had reserved.

It was thirst that awoke us, and it was misery. I took

Madi's hand and led her to the darkened streets. She was still silent, coming to terms with things in her own way. Victor was still missing, so I knew I had to figure this out myself.

"What now, Papa?" Madeline asked.

I looked into her eyes. "Listen to me, love. You are not to harm anyone, understand?"

She made a face. "Why not?"

"Because it's wrong. You mustn't."

"But—it hurts, Papa."

"I know, darling, but you do not need to hurt people for it to cease."

She expressed a pout and crossed her arms in front of her chest. "Hmmph."

I guided her farther down the streets and into an alley. I watched her eyes gather the light and admired the beautiful illumination.

"Look," I said, pointing ahead through the darkness.

"The rats?"

"Yes, love. The rats."

"But…"

"Trust me, Madi. It is the only way."

I lunged forward, effortlessly wrapping my fingers around a scurrying rat. I tore into its throat with my teeth and handed it to Madi. She made another huffing sound but took it from me anyway. She drained it quickly. She dropped it carelessly on the ground, heaving from the feed. She didn't stop there and grabbed rat after rat, tearing them apart.

"Madi, slow down. No need to rush."

"I want more," she whined.

"I think we got them all here."

She huffed again and followed me out of the alleyway to catch a carriage to the manor.

I contacted my new agent, and he promised me the house was ready. I had a European-style manor house for Madeline and me. Not that we needed some place so large, but with my fortune, I couldn't see why not. The house was enormous with towering, black chimneys and peaks that pierced the sky. The balcony was spacious and overlooked the valley. There were fountains and statues in the courtyard, and the interior was just as luxurious, with a white marble entryway and a grand staircase. Each room was filled with beautiful, redwood-framed furnishings and silk rugs. The halls were ordained with stunning paintings. It was perfect. I only wished we could have shared it with Mary.

Madeline walked beside me along the dismal, black streets of the city where, even then, people wandered about. Perhaps the move was for the better. Never in Geneva would there have been so many people about the streets at night. Although, of course, if it hadn't been for the move, this wouldn't have happened to me.

I walked beside my daughter and followed her gaze as she watched a young man dressed in linens, silks, and lace. He had thick golden curls and a small rounded face. He was a charming young boy. I pushed my way into his mind and saw a life so full of love and joy.

Madeline crept closer to the boy as he moved along the street; he was a complete blur of color and movement. It was his beauty and his innocence that captured my attention. I didn't want her to destroy it, but that was what she wanted from him—his silence, his young, flawless features. That's what drew her to him.

"No," I said. "Madeline, don't."

She stared hard at him, and within seconds, she had him pulled into an alley and pinned down upon the ground with her teeth in his throat. She drank quickly, widening the wound with her teeth, almost tearing his head from his body. I froze in place, unable to believe what I was seeing. Finally, I was able to speak.

"That's enough, Madi," I demanded. "Stop."

"I want more."

"You've had enough."

"But I want more."

"We are going home, Madeline. You have to wait."

She huffed but followed me back to the manor. I tried not to think about the boy my daughter had just murdered. I tried to pretend it was just a violent dream—a nightmare. The guilt was gnawing away at me. After all, I was the one who did this to her. Now I had to find a way to fix it.

Our skin was warm from the hunt, but the rat blood in my system was slowly losing its effect. Victor was right. I ached for human blood.

The next night, I ventured out with Madeline. Again, she fed, seeing the humans as nothing more than blood—nothing more than food. I knew I was losing her to something evil inside her—the same evil I was trying to repress in myself. How was I to teach her to respect life the way I did? How could I now change what I had done to her?

"Madi, when we kill, we destroy families. Understand?"

"Yes."

"And do you understand that when you take someone's life, you are doing to them the thing that the monster did to Mama?"

She frowned. "I miss Mama."

"So do I. You must understand. The people you are hurting are not only the ones you kill, Madi. You are hurting their families too."

"But we must, Papa. We must feed."

"But we should still feel sorry. We should still seek forgiveness."

"I do not understand."

I sighed. "I will show you, Madi. And I will find the monster that took Mama away from us. I promise you."

"Why must we find him?" she asked. "We cannot find him, Papa, not any easier than we can hide from him."

"We do not need to hide, Madi."

She didn't respond, just continued down the streets. My eyes caught sight of a very lovely woman strolling down the street. She was clearly wealthy, dressed in the finest. Her silk dress moved gracefully as she walked, and her neck glistened from a string of diamonds about her beautiful throat—the throat I wished to tear into.

"Her?" I heard Madeline ask.

"No," I retorted. "No, I won't hurt her."

"You should," she said.

I tried to ignore her. It was no use. Madi grabbed the woman too fast for mortal eyes to see. I followed her quickly, hoping to stop her.

I watched as my daughter fed viciously, drinking in her fill.

"Here, Papa," she said. "Try some."

I shook my head. "I can't."

"She's already dead, Papa. You didn't hurt her."

My chest burned with regret and guilt for what I had done to her. This was not the Madeline I knew. Yet, even as I knew this, I also knew she was right. I could smell the blood, sweet and savory. My body went rigid for a moment as the hunger raged inside me. Before I even knew what I was doing, I held that beautiful woman in my arms, draining the remaining blood from her body. I stood above her, staring at her face. I knew peace in that moment. I knew peace in the taste of blood.

"See?" Madi said. "It's good." She reached down and took the diamonds from the woman's neck.

I glared at her.

"What? She doesn't need it anymore. It only got in my way anyway."

Madeline followed me back home, but I could barely speak. My craving for human blood was growing stronger by the second.

Now that I tasted it, it only made me need it more. There was no way I could resist. Victor was right. I hated that he was right. I wanted to believe I could choose my own fate, but alas, I was a monster. Nothing I could do was going to change that.

As the weeks passed, I could not say how many victims there were. I could not say who any of them were. They were all her—the black-haired beauty Madeline had fed to me. My daughter cared only for the taste of blood. Nothing else mattered to her. But I suffered in silence, overcome with grief, guilt, and remorse. Madeline…felt nothing.

Chapter Five

IT WAS a cold night in early October. I was sleeping soundly when I was disturbed by the feeling of dark energy striking me, making me feel as if I were being electrocuted. It was strong—potent. I knew that wicked presence; it had become almost a part of me.

I opened my eyes to see only darkness. I threw open the curtains of my bedroom, letting in the light of the moon. Could it be? Could it be that the evil murderer had come back to finish his work? No sooner than that question had come to mind that I knew the answer. *Yes!* But my thoughts were interrupted by a voice answering my question.

"No."

I spun on my heels, tortured, nervous. There before me was a white face and hair...the color of smoke.

"You!" I growled.

The images of Mary still and lifeless in her bed came flooding over me...memories of the way my daughter cried. All of it came back, bringing my rage bubbling to the surface. "You evil, murdering bastard." I raised my fists. "Stay away before I rip you to shreds!" My voice swelled. "You're insane!" I screamed in Italian. "Tu sei pazzo!"

I lifted the candle, and his eyes glowed a deep amber that held a promise of evil! My heart pounded and throbbed faster and faster. Through his mind, he sent images into my own. It was Mary's body in the water, covered with worms and larva. Her silken skin was now rotted and hanging from only a few of her bony limbs. Her gorgeous, crystal eyes were now only black pools of water in her skull. Putrid insects infested her and devoured her flesh and rotting muscles. My rage at him returned once more, and I backed away, pressing my fingers into my temples, trying to clear the images.

I dropped the candle to the floor, where the curtains immediately burst into flames. The images at last had ceased, but I remained on the floor, sprawled out upon the silk rug, feeling the heat from the approaching fire. The flames licked at the floor, igniting the rugs and wooden tables. A lamp crashed somewhere, but I paid no mind. I knew I deserved this now. I deserved to suffer. I deserved every bit of pain I was about to endure. I could hear the crackling of the flames as they inched closer and closer to me. My body ached from the heat, and darkness took me.

I awoke in terrible pain, but the heat had diminished. I opened my eyes and looked around. I didn't recognize the room I was in and could not remember how I had gotten there. It was cold and bare. The walls were nothing but stone. I was lying in a massive bed with thick curtains hanging from posts. I placed a hand on my forehead.

Where the hell am I?

I heard a dark ringing voice, one that could only belong to an immortal. No human possessed such lyrical tones in simple words.

"You are safe," I heard.

I squinted, trying to see better in the darkness. "Who are you?"

"You know who I am."

My face grew hard for a moment, and the feelings of anguish and rage bubbled up from the depths of me. He moved closer, and the moonlight from the window illuminated his face. I saw that smoke-colored hair, and I knew. "You—it's you. You killed my wife."

"I did."

I sprang from the bed and flung myself forward, gripping his neck in my hands.

He laughed tauntingly and moved away from me as if I had no strength at all.

"Why?"

"You are not ready for the answer to that question."

"I have to know."

"You can't understand. Not until you can understand the ways of our kind. Not until you can accept the unchangeable torment of immortality."

"But I do understand," I argued. "I know what I am. I know I am evil. I've killed. I've killed many, and I will

43

kill many more. I was turned into a monster. I have been condemned by a fiend on a ship. I understand it all."

"Then you understand nothing."

My rage returned, and I clenched my hands into fists, wanting to tear into him like a wild animal. I knew I couldn't. He was too strong. I could feel his power emanating from him, vibrating the empty air around me.

"Look for me again," he said. "On a night of ice."

How I despised him. How I wished I could tear him apart with my bare hands and make him suffer as I suffered, make him burn in Hell for taking my sweet Mary! This was what I had wanted. I wanted to find him. I wanted to confront him, and now—I wished I hadn't. I was no match for him.

Look for him on a night of ice. For what? An explanation? A threat? I pushed it aside, trying to pretend as if I had never encountered him, for my fury was making me sick. It was driving me near mad.

I spent an entire year tormented at the feeling of that presence constantly upon me. That tremor in the atmosphere—I couldn't stand it! I would follow it, but it would disappear within seconds.

Victor was right; I did blame him for my misery, and I cursed him every minute of my life.

My daughter had become a vengeful killer, destroying all in her path. She frightened me. The harder I tried to help her hold on to her mortal nature, the crueler and colder she became. She had even ceased to call me Papa.

How was it that *I* was cursed? Why was *I* damned? Why me? There must be a reason, a reason for all this… evil. I thought back to something Victor had said to me. *When you are unstable, find someone who can hold you.* But Madeline wouldn't hold me now, would she? She hated me for the guilt I felt for our victims. She hated the humanity in me. She cared for nothing but the pursuit of blood.

I wished I could leave her—live alone with my suffering. She wasn't my daughter anymore, but when I looked at her, I remembered my Madeline, the child that was the only piece of Mary I had left.

We rented hotel rooms for a while after that fiend had burned down my house. I was sitting alone in the foyer, wallowing in my guilt as I so often did.

Everything that has happened is your fault, Victor. I hate you for what you have done to us.

"Perhaps it is fault of your own, Father," Madeline said, stepping into the room.

"Don't do that," I sighed. "Stay out of my head."

She shrugged. "I just think your pain is your own fault. If you would just accept what we are, it would be easy—fun even. Just let go. Death is a thing that just happens to humans. It is unstoppable. What difference does it make if we kill them or if time kills them? They're all doomed anyway."

"Leave me alone," I said. "I don't want to hear your prattle right now."

"Fine. But you know I'm right."

"Why do you hate me so?" I asked, looking up into her soft green eyes.

"I don't." She took a few steps toward me. "It is not you I hate, Father. It is your mortal coil that is hindering you from your potential."

"Potential?"

"You could be so powerful if you wanted—unstoppable. We both could."

"That's not what I want, Madi."

"No. You want to be human. But you aren't human. You know that. Nothing you can do about it."

I don't know how I knew, but something told me I was losing her to more than her vampire nature. I sighed, finding no words of protest. "You're leaving, aren't you?"

She turned away from me. "Perhaps," she said, sauntering out of the room.

I let her go, not having the strength to argue. I didn't want to be human. I just wanted it to make sense to me. I tried to recall the life I had given up, the colors, the sunlight—all the things that made life what it was. There was no sense to be made of something so dark. I didn't choose this life, but it had found me anyway. Madeline was right about one thing. I couldn't change it. I was born of the night. Didn't I have a right to be what I was?

I knew my daughter was leaving me, and I wondered why I wasn't weeping uncontrollably. She was still a child. Where was she to go? It didn't matter. I knew I could find her again. My blood had bonded us; I could always find her.

I slept that day, knowing that I would indeed wake alone—and I did, without even a note from her. Her bed

—empty. I wept then, whimpered like a lost child. Suddenly, my tears stopped as that presence came again, the evil presence. A rush of random notes, meaningless notes, as if somebody had placed their arms upon the keys of a piano—sharp, sour notes and that heartbeat again, that loud, pounding heartbeat. I sprang to the window, and in an instant—the feeling was gone. I was being followed, being watched. I knew it would return—he wanted me!

Blood I was to find that night. I walked the streets and came to a house that reeked with the scent of mortals. *A party!* I thought. *How wonderful. A party filled with beautiful, colorful creatures and a ballroom full of dancing beauties.* I could hear the conversations of these beautiful mortals and even secret thoughts of love and hate. I could see their faces in my mind and their delicate dancing figures, but I pushed it all aside, remembering I had come for blood.

I still had enough strength to bring myself to the top window of the house. There, I found myself in a dark room. The music had quieted; I heard the sound of foot-steps and the faint whisper of a heartbeat. I hid behind a cedar dresser as the light turned on. I looked at her slowly entering the room, tall and slender with thick black hair in perfect ringlets, her sapphire eyes much like my own. I pushed my way into her mind, listening to her thoughts.

Daniel's waiting for me. I'd better hurry and find that letter. My God, he's beautiful!

She laughed out loud and moved toward a desk, shuffling through a mess of scattered paper.

Where is it?

I wanted so badly to reveal myself, to let her know I was there, but I couldn't. I knew the feeling deep in my gut all too well. I wanted her—her essence, her life…her blood. I tried to ground myself and hold back the urges. Not her. Anyone but her. She was too beautiful.

It was to no avail. I wanted her, had to have her. My body moved on its own without my consent. I hurled myself toward her, readying myself for the kill. My body collided with hers, sending her flying into the cedar dresser, bashing her head on the edge.

Blood gushed from an open wound in her head. The crimson puddle widened and glistened in the moonlight. I smelled the sweetness of the blood—saw it drying on her silken curls. I ached to feed, to taste the salt, the metal, the ecstasy. I licked at the wound, but my body needed to break through flesh, to find the blood myself. I pressed my lips to her neck, but I heard a voice that disturbed me and a knock at the door.

"Rayne?" I heard. "Rayne, are you in there, darling?"

Daniel, I thought. The party was all waiting for her. "Damn you!" I grumbled in a whisper.

I knew I couldn't be found. I looked back at her longingly, wanting her.

"Sorry, darling!" I said and sprang to the window.

My mind haunted me with the sight of that bleeding

girl on the floor. *Dio Mio, I can't just leave her like that.* Should she suffer because of my ill fate? If I truly wanted to be good, I couldn't let her die.

I came back to that room to find her barely alive. I could feel her heartbeat slowing down, and my body begged for her life. I moved toward her. I gripped her hair in my fingers and bit through the soft flesh of her neck.

I was frantic now; she stood on the very brink of death. Hating what I was with every fiber of my being, I broke the vein in my wrist and pressed it to her lips.

"Drink," I said. "Drink!"

Chapter Six

I TRIED to tell her that it was all right, that she would make it through this terrifying transformation. "Va bené," I said. "Va bené."

She didn't hold back as she drank from me, and with each swallow, the gash in her skull began to shrink and completely close. Beautiful white flesh covered the healed bone, and slowly, her magnificent curls began to grow from the newly-formed skin. She knew me now as I knew her. She knew everything I was as soon as the blood began to flow.

She was strong, loving, loyal, strong-willed, intelligent—and oh so beautiful.

When at last I pulled away, I was in great pain and weakness. I had not yet fed that night and was drained far too much. I writhed on the bloody floor of that room, and I saw her beautiful satin curls grow tighter, shinier, and more lucent. The coloring of her eyes brightened and shone with a vibrancy no human could know. Her canine teeth grew ever longer and sharper.

I stayed on that floor, moaning a little from the pain.

The woman bent over me and leaned down, kissing me gently on my hungry lips. I could feel her soft newborn vampire flesh upon my own, and I loved it. I gave a slight orgasmic shudder as she filled my mouth with her hot, fiery blood. She pulled away, and at last I was able to sit up and gaze at my newborn princess.

I was weak yet still aware of the eerie silence and the perfume of roses and youth. I felt no age in her, saw no age in her eyes. She was new, just born—mine.

It was strange to me and quite unexpected when Rayne grasped my hand and pulled me to my feet that she didn't seem frightened or confused. It was like she already understood what she was—what I had turned her into. We walked silently back to the hotel.

"It is a miraculous thing," she started.

"Do not speak of it," I said. "I don't want to think about it."

"I don't understand."

I turned away, staring at the bland, white walls. "I did it to save you," I whispered.

"I know. You're a hero."

"A hero? Are you mad? Don't you understand I would have never had to save you if I could have controlled myself? If I wasn't this…thing—this…monster."

"You are not a monster, Adam Gold."

"Why is it you are not angry? Why are you not frightened or confused?"

She shrugged. "I don't know. When you…after you bit me…"

"When I fed you?"

"Yes. It happened when you fed me your blood. I saw everything. I know what we are and what we must do. And I know you—strong, arrogant, stubborn...and wonderful." She smiled softly and gazed intently into my eyes like she was studying me.

"Why are you looking at me like that?"

"I am simply admiring you."

I smiled. "You're different."

"If you say so," she answered, moving closer, closing the space between us. She wrapped her arms around my neck. "I saw it," she said. "What happened to you...on the ship. I'm so sorry."

I shook my head. "I can't..."

"Adam, the same thing happened to you when you were turned. All the knowledge and answers you had were released into you."

"Then why did I feel so confused? So lost?"

"Because you fought it," she said. "I saw that too. You pulled away from it and pushed it out with every bit of strength you had."

"I didn't want to be this monster. But deep down, I think I knew what was happening. The words came to me, and I did push them away. I submerged myself in denial."

She nodded. "And now?"

"Now—I don't know. I am just me."

"And that's good enough."

I knew something was going to happen that night. I felt uneasy—disturbed. I wanted to ignore it, but I couldn't. Something had me frightened.

I looked at Rayne. The guilt overflowed inside me, the memory of her skin, the warm taste of her blood.

"I feel it too, Adam," she said. "The tremor in the atmosphere." She paused and reached out a delicate, white hand to touch my face. "My hero."

I sighed. "Don't. Do not speak again of making creatures like ourselves. I did it to save you."

"In the end, you did it because you wanted to. I was lonely too."

"Were you?"

"Very much so."

"Then who is Daniel?"

She laughed in a soft, ringing voice that almost sounded like music. "He is just a boy. A twenty-two-year-old, spoiled, rich boy."

"Do you love him?"

"Love? No. I think he may have loved me, but…"

"But what?"

"I didn't feel the same way. There was something missing. There was something I was seeking that I did not find in him."

"What was that something?" I asked.

"Passion. I want to love and be loved with a fire that burns through me—that consumes me and takes me to places I never dreamed existed. I crave adventure and magic, Adam. I was looking for what I found in you."

I was taken aback for a moment, unsure how to respond.

"It's you," she said. She leaned forward, staring into my eyes for a moment.

I stared back, admiring the perfect clarity of the blue hue in hers. She wrapped her arms around my neck, pressing her perfect lips to mine. I wove my fingers through her petal-soft curls and let myself fall weak in her arms.

As her lips moved with mine, I thought of Mary. I remembered her touch, her kiss, and this was not it. I felt a sting of betrayal, and I pulled away, hiding my face in my hands.

"Adam?"

"I'm sorry. I can't…"

"It's all right. I understand."

"There is something happening tonight," I said, turning away, staring out the window into the darkness.

"You feel it too?" she asked. "The tremor in the air?"

"Yes, I feel it."

"What are you going to do?"

"I'm not sure yet, but I need to go. Alone."

She nodded. "Do what you must."

I knew it was that night. I walked along the dark, damp streets alone to clear my mind from the night's kill. I heard the rhythmical tapping of footsteps behind me, moving in unison with my own. I spun around immediately to see no one there. I heard that resonance again—that terrible, stinging sound of misplaced notes and that heartbeat, smooth and lyrical.

It can't be. This is not a night of ice.

But the presence remained, steady and constant, unwavering.

"Show yourself!" I demanded, unsure my calls would be heeded.

My body trembled, and the blood sweat formed in beads upon my forehead. That heartbeat was one of an immortal. I could almost feel his age—eons of it.

"Show yourself, you coward!"

Through the darkness, a shadow emerged, and there it was—that white face, with hair the color of smoke. I gasped and stumbled, almost falling over.

"You!" I whispered in a crackled voice, too soft for him to have heard it if he were mortal. He threw his head back laughing, showing off his pointed teeth, the sudden change in his expression frightening me.

He walked slowly toward me as my rage boiled

within. I began screaming and flailing my arms, unable to hold back. "Wicked monster!" I yelled. "Devil!" I reached for him and struck him hard in the face. I felt the firmness of his body as I began pounding him with my fists over and over as hard as I could. He didn't yield. He stood unfazed and unharmed.

"Leave me, you devil!" I yelled again, cursing him. "Damn you to Satan's fires!"

His face was blank, and I began hitting him again, trying to make his expression change, trying to see one flicker of life. The utter stiffness of his features was maddening.

He seized my wrist. The strength startled me, and my muscles stiffened. I tried to struggle from his grasp, but I was still now. There was a kind of comfort in his presence, a comfort I didn't want him to sense I felt; it wouldn't allow me to move.

"Release me!" I growled through clenched teeth. "Release me from your poisonous hands!"

His brown eyes were not averted from my face, and I continued to look away, frightened of his ageless eyes. I sensed his power stifling the very air, shaking the foundation of the earth I stood upon. His potency was unlike anything I had ever felt before. Oh, what he could teach me...what he could show me. I halted my thoughts, resentful of my weakness. *What am I saying? This monster murdered my darling wife; I am here to destroy him.*

I began to struggle again, feeling the pressure of his hand on my wrist, feeling his power shaking the very ground on which I stood. His strength emanated from his body and passed through me, making me shudder, and my teeth chattered violently. He held his grip on me with ease. His strength was overwhelming. I wanted to be closer to him, to absorb that power, to feel his strength. I wanted to embrace him with my weakened arms, but then my memory flashed with that terrible night on the ship. I began to weep again, and the vampire's expression still did not change.

"You!" I growled. "It was you, you wicked, evil fiend!"

"Evil—yes!" he replied, his voice thick and soft like velvet, with a heavy darkness that rang through me. "But also very beautiful," he continued, with a slight half smile.

I tried to pry my way into his mind, but he was too strong. The only things I would know would be those he wanted me to.

"Murdering bastard," I said, seething. "I wish I could destroy you with one blow."

"Calm yourself," he replied softly.

He placed his hand over my mouth, and I flung it away—he let me.

"First, I must ask you to listen to my reasoning, and then if you still want to kill me, and if you can, then do it. Just remember I am older than you and stronger than you!"

He frightened me to the very marrow of my bones, but I would not let him see it.

"Tell no one of our meeting," he said. "I am glad I have found you. I've been looking for you—as I am sure you know."

"Of course," I replied angrily.

"My name is Relone Akar. There is much to tell, and the sun isn't far. Meet me here tomorrow night, and you will understand. Keep this to yourself, young one!"

I wanted to be infuriated and scream at him until I lost my voice, but he was gone before I could blink. I pressed my fingers to my temples to calm the confusion. I tried to move from the street corner, but I remained there for many minutes where his presence still lingered. When the sensations dissipated, I walked back to the hotel. When I arrived, Rayne was sleeping with a coloring in her cheeks, warm from the night's kill. I slept beside her through the daylight hours.

I awoke late when the sky was dark. Rayne turned to me and smiled. There was no denying her beauty, but there was more to it when she looked at me that way. I reached for her, yearning to feel her skin against mine. I touched her cheek, and she laid her hand upon mine, moving it to her lips. I placed my forehead against hers, feeling suddenly weak and powerless against the affection I felt toward her.

She hoisted herself up, pressing her lips to mine. The kiss was deep and passionate. She parted her lips, and the realization of what I was doing finally hit me. I pulled away harshly. I got up from the bed, unsure of what it meant and a little embarrassed.

"Adam, are you all right?" she asked.

"I'm all right."

"What—what just happened?"

"Nothing," I said, turning back to face her.

"What do you mean?"

"It was nothing, Rayne. It was a moment of weakness. Neither of us are very good at being alone."

I saw something flicker across her eyes. I couldn't be sure, but it resembled pain, like what I said hurt her. I never intended to hurt her. I should not have been surprised she had fallen in love with me. Everyone did.

I could not let that kiss mean anything. I refused. I still felt married, felt as if my wife was seeing this and cursing my betrayal.

"I'm worried about you, Adam."

"Don't be," I answered. "I'm all right. I promise."

"You trouble your mind too much, my darling."

"Do I?"

"I suppose I wouldn't know. I can read your thoughts, Adam, yet I am unsure why you hate Relone as much as you do."

"He's a murderer!" I cried.

"Have you listened to him yet, my darling?"

"Are you mad?" I yelled. "Why would I want an explanation? Why do I need a reason to hate him? He murdered my wife, Rayne. That is enough of a reason to hate anybody—is it not?"

She sighed. "Yes. It is, Adam. I'm just troubled."

"Why?"

"Because of what might happen. Because you have so much hatred and so much anger inside of you. It can drive you mad!"

"I'm all right," I said, trying to calm her. I could feel her concern. "I just need to accomplish this…task. Once I kill Relone, then I don't care what happens to me. But—Adam—I do care what happens to you."

I shunned her. I walked away, and she followed me. "I want to be alone," I told her. "I mean not to hurt you. I am just having far too many thoughts to burden you with." I grabbed my jacket and headed for the door, eager to get away. The night was cold, and frost clung to the shingles on the nearby buildings—a night of ice.

As I walked the streets, he appeared in front of me as if he were made from the darkness itself. Again, I could feel his power, and it brought a sense of urgency into my bones. I felt drawn to him, seduced by his strength.

"I know what you think of me," he said, reminding me again the preternatural sound of his voice. My memory never did it justice.

"That you're an evil murderer with a heart full of hate?"

"I do not hate you," he told me. "In fact, I am quite fond of you."

"Of course you are, but you are a murdering son of a bitch, and it is taking every ounce of energy I possess to not hurl myself toward you and sink my teeth into your neck."

He smiled. "I know."

"I want to kill you."

"But you haven't tried yet."

"I am waiting for you to tell me why you did what you did. I have to know, Relone. I cannot kill you until I know."

He smiled. "Do you think you can kill me, Adam Gold?"

"I think my hatred for you is strong enough."

"I think your love for me is stronger."

"Love? Now wait just a minute."

He laughed again.

"I have hardly spoken to you, and even if I had, there

is no way I could ever love you. Don't you understand what you have done to my life?"

"Of course I do, young one," he answered. "But if I hadn't done what I did, your life would be even more wretched than it is now. You are the one that is hurt for reasons he does not understand!"

I clenched my hands into fists.

"I can tell you are drawn to me—you ache for me."

"It isn't love."

"But nor is it hate."

"I wouldn't be so sure."

"Love and hate," he started. "They are quite similar."

"What are you talking about?" I yelled. "Are you mad?"

I sighed and turned away, staring at the flickering flame of the street lamp. I couldn't look at him. His age was making me uneasy. I stood up from the curb, and he mirrored my movement.

"I want to listen to you," I said. "I want an explanation, Relone. Then I can kill you, and my life will be fine. After I kill you, I do not care what happens to me. Whether I live or die, I do not care."

"Love and hate," he said again shaking his head. He leaned against the lamppost and crossed his arms in front of his chest. He looked very human standing there. Only, his skin was glowing more than usual from the light. He was a silent, passive person it seemed. He thought more than he spoke. Perhaps he was simply not saying what he wanted—what he needed.

"I am saying what I want," he answered.

His response startled me. "Stop doing that!" I demanded.

"I apologize," he said. "I will tell you now what I want to say and what I feel I need to say."

I nodded.

"I say that love and hate are similar. You are confused by that. Love and hate are opposite of one another. They do not coincide, correct?"

"Stop reading my thoughts!"

"I am not reading your thoughts, Adam. I am asking you—is that what you are thinking?"

"Yes…"

"Then let me explain."

"Yes…"

"You hate yourself because you love me."

"What?"

"Love and hate in the same situation. You hate me because you love me, and you hate yourself because you love me. You love and hate me the same as you love and hate yourself. You see? Love and hate in the same situation…"

"I do not hate myself, and I do not love you. You are mistaken on two accounts, if not more than that."

"You love yourself, yes, which is obvious. You are an arrogant, potent creature, Adam, and yet you hate yourself at the same time."

"Why do you say that?"

"How do you feel about Miss Cunningham?"

"Who?"

"The woman you killed tonight, whose blood quenched your thirst?"

"I feel…"

"You feel guilt—regret. You hate yourself for what you must do. Am I right?"

"You honestly need to stop invading my mind, Relone."

He laughed. "You are so naïve, Adam."

"How so?"

"I have barely read your thoughts. Everything you feel is so apparent in the way you look at me. The way you sigh when you are thinking silently to yourself. The way you fold your hands in front of your stomach and stare at the ground, the way you clench your fists and grind your teeth when you are angry. It is not difficult to read you. Whether I am reading your thoughts or not, I know what you are thinking. I can see what you are feeling."

"That distresses me," I said. "Not even my feelings are my own."

"What is the use of thoughts and feelings if you have nobody to share them with?"

I stared at him, looking very confused.

He laughed. "Don't look at me that way." He sighed and looked away from me to the dark street in front of him. "Love and hate."

"Stop saying that," I said calmly, not averting my eyes from the darkness ahead. "It's bothering me."

"I apologize," he said. "You wanted to listen to me, so I was speaking."

"I want my explanation now."

"Soon."

"Soon? You have been saying soon for a long time now, Akar!"

"Relax," he answered, looking at me. He shifted his weight from the lamppost to his feet and put his hands on my shoulders. He leaned his forehead against mine. "Soon," he whispered.

I sighed and stared into his eyes.

"Soon. I promise."

I nodded, and within a second, he was gone. I hated the way he did that, leaving before I had a chance to respond to him. I wanted to tell him… What *did* I want to tell him? Perhaps it didn't matter. Perhaps that is why he left.

When I arrived back at the hotel, Rayne was sitting up in bed, reading a paperback novel. The oil lamp was on beside the bed as if she couldn't see. She was dressed in a white silken nightdress where I could see the tresses of her body—her perfect body. I smiled and crawled into bed beside her.

"What did he say?" she asked me.

"What? What did who say? I went out for food."

"Yes, I know that. But you saw Relone tonight, did you not?"

I sighed. "Yes…"

"You look relieved, Adam."

"I will be soon. I will listen to him, and then—I will kill him."

"Sleep, my love," she said. "You have exhausted yourself with all this talk of hate and evil."

I nodded. "I know. Sleep may help. Our curses are the same, my lovely."

"What nonsense are you saying?" She set the book down on the nightstand.

"We share the same curse, Rayne—the most wretched of all curses. We are immortal blood hunters. We are creatures who should have never come into existence in the first place."

"You cannot help what you are, Adam." She turned off the lamp and lay down, looking into my blue eyes. She kissed my forehead. "Vampire or mortal—I love you the same."

"Curse or no curse—we are dead."

Chapter Seven

"YOU WANT HIM, DON'T YOU?" she started, scattering my thoughts.

"What do you mean?" I asked coldly, feeling as tense as she did.

"You are drawn to him as he is drawn to you. He wants you as a companion to share eternity with. I can read your thoughts, Adam—I know!"

"You are my child," I said. "I made you like me to save you. I am bonded to you, not Relone.

She didn't reply, but she was right. I knew he wanted me, but I couldn't let my infatuation with his potency drive me to him, accepting him—forgiving him. I wouldn't. There was nothing he had to offer me. Nothing but pain.

"Adam?" Rayne asked me, making me aware of her presence.

"Yes...?"

"The carriage. It's here."

I nodded. "Give me a moment."

My new house was finally ready and even more luxurious than the one that had burned to the ground. No more rented hotel rooms.

I placed my elbows on the keys of the piano, ignoring the wretched sound. I laid my chin in my hands and sighed.

What am I doing here? I thought. *Why am I not out burning that murdering bastard like a torch?*

"Adam!" Rayne called.

"I'm coming, darling!" I grabbed our bags by the door and followed her out to the carriage.

The driver looked at me suspiciously when I paid him much more money than I owed him. I was hoping it wasn't my eyes that had caught his attention. I hated always feeling like I didn't belong. But I didn't, did I? I didn't belong anywhere. It had never been any different for me, not since Victor had cursed me.

I stared at my house when we arrived. A black wrought iron gate surrounded the property. The house took up a ridiculous amount of space, which suited me perfectly. It was three stories, which was, of course, unnecessary. It was a white house with a red tiled roof; the tops of two of the towers were a pale yellow color. There were three balconies visible in just the front of the house.

"What are you doing?" Rayne asked me. "Counting windows, my darling?"

I smiled.

"Don't worry." She laughed. "It is exactly what you asked for. I'm sure of it."

I smiled again. Yes, it was exactly what I asked for. There were windows everywhere and double doors in the front. There was a lovely courtyard with a fountain directly in the center, traditional, which is what I liked.

I walked inside and instantly grinned. The entry way was white tile and large enough to be a ballroom. I looked at Rayne in her dark green gown and imagined her in a dress of scarlet red spinning in my embrace to soft, lovely music. I could almost feel her in my arms as I looked up at the crystal chandelier above my head that enchanted me quite a bit.

"It's lovely," she said.

"It is."

I looked to the winding staircase—the grand staircase, one might call it. Above the railing stood a lovely painting—a scene of young mortals in a coffee house. I smiled. There were rugs of many colors in every room. It was furnished with pieces of great beauty and value, silver and gold everywhere. I am Adam Gold. I would not settle for less.

That night, I didn't sleep well. My mind haunted me with my hatred for that ancient creature, Relone. More than hating Relone, I hated myself for not truly hating him. I tied back the curtains of my dark-colored canopy. I wasn't cold. Would never really be cold. I snuggled close to my lovely Rayne and tried my best to fall asleep.

Sleep found me eventually as it often did when I least expected it. I awoke before the sun went down and couldn't fall back asleep. I lay there wrapping Rayne's curls around my fingers until she woke.

"Darling?"

She smiled. "Sleep well?"

"I wouldn't say so," I answered, "but I'm all right."

"Are you sure?"

I nodded. "May I ask you something?"

"Of course," she answered with a melodic tone in her voice.

"What do you think about God?"

"What?" She laughed.

"God. What do you think of him?"

"Well...I don't."

"You don't *ever* think about God?"

"Why should I?"

"I don't know," I answered. "Because it's natural."

"Is it?"

"Victor told me not to turn to God when I am unstable. He told me to turn to someone who would hold me."

She smiled and embraced me. "If you wanted me to hold you, all you had to do was ask."

I laughed. "No," I said, moving away from her and leaning against my pillow. "I really want to know what you think about God."

"I told you. I don't." She took a book off the shelf beside her. "I simply don't. Why should I think about God? He is nothing to me but an idea."

"Is he?"

"You are asking me?"

"Is that really what you believe, Rayne?"

"Is it not what you believe, Adam?"

"I am so confused, darling, that I don't know what I believe."

She sighed. "I worry about you."

"There is no reason to. I assure you."

The world was changing. I could feel it. It was like I could literally feel Earth spinning faster and the winds changing direction. It was a new era.

Rayne came to sit beside me on the loveseat in the front room. "I think you need to go to him."

"What?"

"Relone. I think you need to go to him."

"I will," I answered. "I am still waiting for his explanation."

"That's not what I mean."

"What are you saying?"

"Adam—you're miserable. I see it day by day. You suffer."

"Yes. Because of him!"

"No," she said calmly. "Because of you. Because of what you are. Because you need answers. You long for them."

"Do I?"

"Don't you?" She grasped my hand. "Don't you want to know how you came to be this way? And why?"

"And you believe he can tell me these things?"

She smiled at me, her blue eyes beaming. "So do you."

"I feel drawn to him," I said, breaking my gaze from

her eyes. "I won't deny that. But there is hatred there, Rayne. Anger and pain. I cannot let myself want him."

"But you *do* want him, Adam. Do not fool yourself. Do what you need to do."

"I cannot leave you."

"Yes, you can," she said, tears building in her eyes. "It's all right. I will see you again. You know that."

I shook my head. "It hurts you. I will not do it if it hurts you."

"It's all right," she said again, touching my face. "You need him, Adam. As I needed you. Go to him."

"Dio Mio," I murmured. "Why must I need the one person who destroyed my life?"

"Listen to him and you might know."

I sighed, placing my head in my hands, unable to respond.

Chapter Eight

I WAS STILL aware of the longing I felt for the potent and beautiful Relone Akar. I knew if I didn't get as far away from him as possible, I would fall weak to that longing. I was more terrified then of succumbing to my weakness than not exacting my revenge.

"I don't want to hurt you," I said to Rayne. "I don't wish to leave you."

"But you're not being fair to yourself," she replied. "I understand it better than you think. I happen to be the only connection you have to your time and your era. The years are passing. I feel it too. I feel like this era is closing in upon us. You don't want to forget these times or feel as though they never existed."

"Yes."

"But, my love, the times change. You need to be in touch with the world now. You need to finally let go of your mortal years. I have. You're still my hero."

I felt as if there was more that she wanted to tell me,

but she resisted. I walked away from her. I meant to. I didn't want the words forced from her.

"Tell me," she started. "What was it like—having a family?"

I thought about it for a moment, remembering Mary and the pain of what I had done to Madeline. I had gone so long without thinking about my daughter. I knew I would not be able to keep the pain buried otherwise. I put up that barrier in my mind to keep the memories to myself.

"Words can't really describe it," I said. "It is something I miss."

"Why can't you just tell me how it came to be that I am your only companion? Why have you not given the dark blood to another? Why do you believe such a thing to be evil?"

"Please, Rayne. I can't."

I turned away again. I was scrambling now, in a rush and desperate to leave the feeling of Relone far away. If I didn't, I knew I could never escape the need to be with him.

"Hurry, darling," I said as she began to speak again. I didn't know what she was saying. "The carriage is here. Get your hat."

I opened the door, and she grasped my wrist. Such unexpected strength startled me. I was expecting her to yell, yet she was calm. Her face was not expressionless; she looked—sad, as if tears would spring from her gentle eyes at any moment. I slowed my gestures to liquid-like and turned, as to stare straight through her, to listen to her with every part of my being. I put my hands on her shoulders.

"Tell me, please," she pleaded. "Tell me truly why you don't want to leave me."

I sighed. "I will tell you the reason, the truth, only—I am not sure it is really what I'm feeling."

"It would hurt me more if you were to tell me nothing at all."

"You are all I have ever known since Victor gave me the dark blood. You're right. I don't want to lose the connection to my times, my age. As the years pass, I fear I may forget. Relone has told me he is evil—and he is guiltless. I want that, Rayne."

"You want to lose your guilt?"

"Yes," I whispered solemnly. "I want so badly to let go of my regret. I want to live knowing that it's all right to be what I am, that I can't change it. The only problem is that I do not believe I can let you go. I will miss you far too much."

"You must," she whispered. "You must just let me go. Once you do, you will feel that freedom Victor promised you."

She smiled through her pain and placed a rosary around my neck. I looked down at it.

"To remember me," she said. "Now go, my love."

"As if I could ever forget you," I whispered.

I knew she was right. I knew that Relone needed me to save him now, that he needed a companion lest the lonely centuries would drive him to his death, but I still could not let go of the hate I felt toward him. How could I ever be free and guiltless by being mentored by the man who murdered my wife? How could that possibly be right? The hold he had over me was too strong to deny. Rayne was right. It was time.

I left to find Relone waiting for me at the street corner where he always was, just after the streetlights had been lit.

"I cannot tell you how glad I am to have met you," he said, speaking softly as if to a friend. "I am thankful I have lived long enough to find you. I know you are still angry—confused. There are many things an immortal your age has left to learn."

I could feel his power as I always had. As much hate as I felt, there was also comfort. I almost wanted him to embrace me, to weep for my pain in his arms.

"I would like to teach you those things if you will let me."

"I am unsure anyone can help me now," I said. "There is too much guilt, regret."

"You are young and naïve," he said. "You think you have suffered? You don't know suffering."

A ping of fear shook through me. "Are you threatening me?"

"Of course not," he said, still calm. "I am telling you the truth. You have been lucky, my friend. More than you know. I do not wish to harm you. I want to help you, to prevent any more pain from coming to you."

"Why should I believe you? After what you did?"

"I need you to trust in me and understand. I need to know that you are able to forgive me for what I have done."

"I don't believe I can do that," I answered, staring at the golden glow of his tense eyes.

"Until you are sure you can, I cannot help you."

Every gesture was so sudden and unexpected in his face that every time he blinked or smiled, it startled me. I didn't know if I could do this. He listened to me the way people dream of being listened to, and he cared about what I had to say. A choice needed to be made.

"I need time," I told him.

"Very well. Time is one thing we have an abundance of." I saw the shadow of a smile pull at the corners of his lips. "You know where to find me."

Rayne was still there when I returned, and I felt more overjoyed to see her than I anticipated. That lasted only until she said the same maddening words she had before.

"You're back."

"Of course."

"I wasn't sure you would come back."

"I wasn't sure you would still be here. I meant what I said. I don't want to leave you."

"I know," she said, closing the book she was reading.

I came to sit beside her and put my arm around her delicate shoulders.

"He can give you answers—answers that I never could."

"I care for you," I said. "I tried not to, but it was no use. I cannot just walk away now. Not after all this."

"That's just it," she said. "If you stay, I could never forgive myself for letting my heart hold you back."

"It's my choice."

"Then this is mine."

"Please don't say that," I begged.

"It's time, Adam. You know it is."

The night came more swiftly than I expected, and I embraced her for a long time, breathing in the fragrance of her youth and feeling her flawless curls against my cheek. My eyes filled with unshed tears as I stood back, staring at her perfect face.

She leaned in, kissing me unexpectedly. I didn't hold back this time and returned it. She parted her lips, deepening the kiss, and her tongue passed between my lips, igniting a sort of passion in me.

Now more than ever, I didn't want to leave her. She pulled away from me, staring into my eyes.

"Goodbye, my blue-eyed beauty."

"Goodbye," I whispered, almost forcing the word from my mouth. "You're still my princess."

"And you're still my hero."

I softly kissed her cheek, tasting her blood tears. Couldn't I stay all night holding her and kissing her? One more night—just one more?

I stared at the gleam of her eyes. She stood there watching me. Was I really that beautiful? That magical? Am I really so wonderful that our parting should cause her to cry like this?

"You're beautiful," I whispered.

She didn't respond, but her thoughts told me the

words I didn't want to hear, though when I heard them, I couldn't help but respond.

"I love you too, darling," I said.

"Go," she whispered, "before it's too late, before my heart holds you back—go!"

I forced my legs to move, and for a moment, my muscles ached with the motion. Rather than leaving with the carriage away from Relone's presence, I walked alone toward him, feeling the tremor in the earth become stronger with every step until I thought I would crumple to the ground.

He wasn't at the street corner, but I could feel he was near. The scent of age and death was in the air. I followed the scent to the graveyard.

As I walked on, I could faintly see shapes in the black night. It was as if the dead had risen from the earth and stood there dueling in the darkness. I approached closer. Of course, it was only Relone, but there was another—a stranger. I stepped closer.

A mortal? I stepped closer, sensing her panic, feeling her fear as if it were my own. Yes, it was surely a mortal. She was lovely. Golden hair and eyes of violet. She was young with smooth, delicate features and still in her nightdress, aroused from an innocent slumber.

My hate for Relone returned, my loathsomeness for what we were.

I felt the coolness of droplets hitting my skin and looked toward the heavens to see it had begun to rain. The girl struggled hopelessly in Relone's grasp, her wet hair flying everywhere. I watched the droplets fall from her dark eyelashes and mingle with her tears. Her wet nightdress stuck to her body, and I could see her in all her beauty. The water ran down her plump little arms and over her perfectly shaped breasts, thin waist, and long legs. She was so beautiful, and I silently pleaded for Relone not to hurt her.

She stood there bathing in her fear and in his eyes. The taste of her flowed through my veins. Relone's gray hair glistened in the light from the moon, looking as though it were gray with age. The girl's yellow hair glowed from the shadow of her pale face. The taste of her blood was on my lips, her salty flesh and the iron of her life. Tears ran down her blushing cheeks. She was silent now, and her tears ceased, the last few dripping off her chin. She knew she was dying. She stared at me as if asking me to help her; she saw my sadness, my regret. Even as a mortal, she could see it, so I knew Relone could as well, and I loathed that fact. Her fear came over me, a tremor, as if the very foundation of the earth had shifted. My sympathy for her made me want to cry out to her, to try and save her. I knew I could do nothing. Relone's strength was too much. There was no other option than to stand there in misery and watch as he destroyed an innocent beauty.

She looked at me longingly. Did I seem beautiful to her too? Did I look like I could save her? I felt if she truly knew who I was, what I was, evil words would bleed from her lips, and there would be no love. I looked at her, telling her she was beautiful, using my mind gift to tell her not to be afraid, telling her there would be no more pain.

Relone moved her long golden hair over her shoulder, revealing her pale neck. He ran his fingers over the major artery, and gently, he pressed his lips to the skin and broke through.

She closed her eyes and let herself go, gave herself over. Her fear was gone now. Relone held her in his arms, and she left peacefully, still thinking of me. I saw her life in my mind and tried not to cry out. The cry would be an ear-shattering scream, one that could break all the glass in the city and possibly even destroy me. Her life was love—so full of love.

I could still taste that love and the blood of that lovely victim. As that tremor left my body and all I felt was Relone, I knew she was dead. He dropped her carelessly upon the dirt.

"My God," I whispered. "And to think you…are as I am."

"You're so innocent," he said, taking in a breath of the icy air. "Don't hate me, young one. Give me a chance to explain, for I have done nothing wrong."

"Nothing?"

"Unless you weren't going to create your wife as an immortal, which I knew you were, I have done nothing wrong!"

I disagreed, and he shunned me.

"Come," he said. "Let me tell you what you have come to hear."

He moved slowly across the graveyard, and I followed. He stopped and turned to me.

"Here?" I asked.

"Look," he said, pushing away a layer of leaves and soil, revealing what looked to be a crypt hidden from humans. He led me down stone steps, where torches hung from the walls, lighting the way.

"You see?" he started. "I live beneath the ground with the bodies of my victims."

"You've built a catacomb?"

"If you would like to call it that, then yes."

"My God," I whispered, hearing my voice ringing in the walls and bouncing off the stone.

I could still taste the girl's blood on my lips, yet now with Relone so near, the shaking fear was gone. There was no terror. I felt so safe there, content, and I hated that. I longed to feel that fear again. I yearned for something to happen, for the stones beneath my feet to crumble, for the rails along the steps to tremble, for the walls of the catacomb to writhe as if in life, anything to cure the silence. I felt as if I were begging some self-invented phantoms to frighten me, to endanger my cursed life, but there was only silence.

Relone's brown eyes stared at me, and I almost ached for his company.

"Does your tale justify murder?" I growled. "Does it —*can* it justify so vile a crime?"

"Do not insult me!" he demanded, sitting on a coffin that lay upon the ground. It was then that I noticed the stench I had not noticed before. He signaled me to the coffin opposite him. "Sit. Let us begin as we should. Not from anger!"

I shook my head. "I'd rather stand."

"Sit," he repeated.

"I'd rather stand," I said again.

"It's a very long tale."

I refused.

"Suit yourself," he answered. "Shall we begin?"

I sighed. "Yes. I am ready to listen."

"I am the oldest living vampire that you are sure to ever meet," he started. "There are others, but I doubt you will ever encounter them. I wish I could have described the love between my maker and me. Was there love between you and your maker?"

"None," I replied.

"There must have been a reason for him to make you."

"He loved the dark gift. He loved that he could produce others as cursed as himself—loved that he had that power."

He nodded in understanding. "I was on that ship with you and Victor. Yes, I knew Victor, loved him too as it were, but when I saw he was going to make you, I knew then of your plans. Your dying daughter, I knew you were waiting to create her to save her and that your wife would be next. Your Madeline had a power that you could not have predicted, and your Mary, as sweet as she was, had a power even stronger than your daughter. I saw that power —that potency. I saw what she would be. Adam, you must understand. A vampire is what she would have been, but a monster is what she would have become. It was her or our race. She would have killed carelessly—ruthlessly, without mercy, exposing us to an unsuspecting world, endangering our very species. Her or all of us."

"Fear?" I questioned in a whisper.

He didn't respond, and my voice rose to a booming shout in the walls of the crypt. "Fear?"

He stood up to defend himself.

"No justice!" I screamed. "Your story does not justify murder!"

"Adam, I am not finished yet!" he yelled. "Her or our

race! Adam, please—I'm not finished yet. For the love of God, listen to me!"

"You!" I screamed. "This is all because of you! All of my suffering, all of my pain!"

"It was her or our race," he said again. He lifted his arms. "Our entire species, Adam!" He stepped forward and said angrily, the same words over and over again. "It was her or our race!"

I didn't back away. I screamed in fury and sank my teeth into his neck in rage.

When I returned to my home, Rayne wasn't there. I didn't sleep much that morning. I wept for a long time before I felt tired. Where had she gone? I knew my blood had bonded us, and I could have found her if I wanted to. However, she was right about me. I did need answers—I needed Relone. I tried to resist, but when I thought about Madeline and what she had become, it started to make sense to me. If Mary was to be even half as cruel and callous as my daughter, she would not have been the woman I loved. It was still difficult to accept. I still loved Mary. That would never change.

It was a week before I decided to return. The previous confrontation had me feeling quite embarrassed. I walked along the streets, concentrating on the cool air against my skin. I halted when I spotted a small child cradling a doll. Her big, round eyes were red, and tears stained her cheeks. I came closer, intent on helping her. She must have been lost. As I approached her, that pity turned to a fiery, burning thirst. Her heartbeat was quick and heavy, and the pumping of her blood called out to me. I reached for her, longing to cradle her, to comfort her. The thirst wanted only to destroy her.

Closer I came until my fingers brushed across her dark hair. The blood still pumping filled my head, and nothing existed but blood. Her blood. I could no longer hold back, and I held her in my arms as my teeth sank into her neck.

I knew peace then. I knew silence, stillness, and joy. Then the guilt came—the gnawing regret at what I had done. I stared at the child now on the ground, her dark hair sprawled out around her. I wasn't even sure I had killed her, and I prayed silently to let her be spared.

"You can't pretend, you fool," I heard in a whisper.

I turned to see Relone.

"Coward."

"I am no coward!" I shouted back, stepping toward him.

"We feed on life, Adam. Not just blood."

"She's just a child."

"That makes no difference."

"Of course it does."

He sighed.

I turned to look again at my victim. Relief crawled into me. I could hear her breathing and the beating of her heart. Thank God she was alive.

"You should not feel so much," Relone said. "You

should not let yourself have so much humanity. It only makes your existence more painful."

"I don't want to be evil," I said. "Can't there be goodness somewhere in this now cursed soul?"

He laughed. "Good?" A long sigh. "You have gifts, my son. You possess mind gifts, speed, strength. You can defy the laws of nature. Why do you have this obsession with love?" He laughed again, and it tainted me. "You are a predator, Adam, but you are not evil!"

"But I am!" I argued. "I know I belong in Hell! I am a sinner. I have killed over and over, and I would do it again!" I cringed when I heard myself speaking those familiar words that had passed through my mind so many times; all those variations of goodness seemed to fade from within me.

"But you're not being fair to yourself," he argued back. "You are a killer. That is what you are. You must accept it. God kills. Nature kills. What makes us any different? Is the wolf evil who kills the hair? Is the coyote evil who kills the fox?"

I pondered those words for a moment. "Your logic is flawed in one way."

"And what way is that?"

"The creatures you mentioned are clearly not evil, but nor have they been transformed into something unnatural."

"And what makes you think we are unnatural? Who are you to know where we truly come from? Good and evil are human concepts, Adam. They do not matter to us."

I didn't reply. I had no words to argue.

He continued. "Do you think we were made to be condemned?"

"Yes!" I confessed strongly. "I do. Yet I was raised to trust in God, and I don't understand how he could—"

"Speak not of God," he interrupted, his tense eyes flashing. "You can't really believe in him, now can you? Heaven? Hell?"

"I don't know anymore," I answered solemnly. "I really don't."

"Oh, Adam," he began, softening. "Sweet blue-eyed Adam."

I sighed. "I would give anything to be human again, Relone. That is what you fail to understand."

"Oh, you are quite wrong," he answered. "I am so very afraid of death. If I wasn't, I would give up everything for only one day of mortality. Of sunlight and a sky that I can see as blue and not black. For the waters to be blue. For the heat of the sun to cause pleasure not pain. Everything for just a few hours or even just a few moments of the wonder I so miss now. Do you know what I would give to enter that doll shop, Adam? To walk in during the day and buy a lovely doll for a child of my own?"

I turned around and looked where he was pointing. The shop was dark and empty, and I understood then, the loss he must be feeling to never have a family.

"I am alone," he said. "Can't you save me from my loneliness? The endless bout of eternity? Without you, I don't know what else I have that would compel me to continue a life."

I was silent.

"Without you, I would be willing to give up all the

eras for one mortal life. I do not hate what I am. I have learned to accept it, but if I am to be alone forever, then what is immortality? What is it besides a meaningless hole of existence? I would rather burn my body to ashes."

I contemplated again, thinking about the child and the black-haired woman I saw in every mortal I killed. Why must we feed on the blood of the innocent? If we were to kill, it should be the ones who do not deserve life? Kill those who are cruel to each other, those who murder, those who steal.

Again, Relone had read my thoughts, which was becoming rather irritating, for I could not close my mind from him.

"Yes," he said. "You have a love like no other. You are right, Adam. Kill the evil."

"Stop doing that."

He ignored and just smiled at me. "Come."

"Where?"

"Hunt with me."

"You want to hunt? Together?"

He nodded. "Come."

We stalked the streets. Most of the mortals I found were innocent in most ways and loved by many. I would not harm them. I had vowed against it.

"Her," Relone said, pointing out an older woman with thick, auburn hair resting in waves upon her shoulders.

"How do you know?"

"Look closer," he said.

I stared at her, following close behind her. I looked into her mind. I knew about the knife she had hidden in the waistband of her dress. I knew about the young woman she planned to slaughter with it.

"Her," I answered.

We stalked her for several blocks until I could wait no longer. I raced toward her, using my speed to pull her away from any spying eyes in the streets. She never even saw me coming.

Chapter Nine

MY HATRED for Relone diminished as we hunted. Little by little, there was a love I was beginning to feel—an understanding and a bond. We searched out the murderers, following them sometimes for days, reading their thoughts and witnessing their deeds.

Relone's hand was warm when he gripped my shoulder. "It will be dawn soon."

I nodded. "I do not wish to stay in the crypt tonight."

"I expected you would say that. That's all right, but I do not feel you should return to your house just yet."

"Why?"

He sighed. "She's not there, Adam."

I moved my eyes away from his face. "I know."

"Going back there—feeling her presence. You would weep for hours."

"I wouldn't," I argued, feeling almost offended by his accusation of my weakness.

"All the same, it's best to not be there tonight."

We entered a hotel a few blocks away, and the scent

of fear assaulted me. There were mortals about, but every single one of them reeked of dread and terror.

Garlic hung about the doorways, and the man at the front counter was wiping his moistened face with a handkerchief, his hands shaking furiously.

Relone looked at me with the same glimmer in his tense, brown eyes.

The man reached into his pocket again to retrieve his handkerchief.

"Look around," Relone said. "The garlic at the doorways, the crucifixes on the walls. There is talk amongst these parts of our kind. Simply superstitions. Don't worry. This will be fun."

I remembered I was still wearing the rosary Rayne had given me. I reached into the neck of my white shirt and revealed the necklace. The clinking beads of the ornament gave me that dreamy sensation of the past and made me miss Rayne terribly. I tried not to think about her now. It was not the time.

The man continued to dab at his face. Relone and I stepped forward, and the man glanced at the rosary around my neck. His eyes softened for a moment.

"What troubles you, sir?" Relone asked him.

"There is talk," he started. His voice was half throttled by his shaking. "Talk of…" He broke off, clearing his throat. "The land behind the city graveyard. The woman known as Emily Conner—she is dead. The people talk. They talk, and they say…" He swallowed and inhaled slowly. His voice fell to a whisper. "Vampires."

Relone laughed, which seemed to startle the man. "Oh, sir, do you truly believe in such creatures?"

He didn't respond.

I held up the rosary I was wearing, and Relone tore a piece of garlic from the entrance.

"You see?" Relone said. "Even if such creatures existed, your hotel is safe from them."

The man was silent for a moment and at last nodded his head.

Relone paid and booked the room for three days.

We walked arm in arm to the room. Relone locked the hotel door behind him and smiled at me.

"Why me?" I asked quietly.

"What?"

"Why did you choose me?"

"Aw, Adam." He chuckled. "Do you not know?"

"I don't."

He laughed. "You just want to hear it, Adam."

"Yes," I laughed. "I suppose I do."

"I love you," he said. "I cannot explain why, but I do. You're a fledgling immortal with a lust for blood the same as my own. I chose you because you are the vampire that everybody wants." He broke off, whirling back toward the door, his eyes as wide as saucers.

"What is it?" I asked, fear creeping into my words.

"Someone is listening," he said.

"Someone—what?"

"We must not speak again of creatures like ourselves," he said. "And we are leaving this place after tonight. By then, everyone in this damned hotel will know what we are!"

The hotel attendants who brought food to our rooms drenched it in garlic and never made eye contact with either one of us.

We left early the following evening.

"We need to be more careful," Relone said. "We need to remember the way we move and the things we say are not normal to mortals."

"I understand," I said. But truly I was dreading having to return to the vile catacomb.

It was a dark night, and the streets were empty. Relone wanted me to hunt alone that night. He felt I needed it. I ached for the taste of innocent blood, the kind evil doers didn't possess.

I entered through an unlocked window, planning to take the sleeping beauty in the bed. I took a few steps forward, and her dark eyes opened. I instantly backed away when I saw her eyes gathering the light and glowing like my own. I silently begged for Relone—wished he were here.

She didn't avert her eyes from my face, and I found myself against the wall. I could feel her strength and her youth filling my body to the very brim. It was as if the earth were shifting over and over.

She stood from her bed. I pressed my back into the wall, unsure of why I was frightened. I tried to read her thoughts, but it caused a terrible, throbbing ache in my head. She slowly stepped toward me, her midnight black hair loose around her shoulders. Her hips moved gracefully, and her silk nightdress hugged her perfect body, accentuating its curves.

She reached out a petite, poreless hand. I shut my eyes, preparing myself for pain. I felt a smooth coolness upon my cheek, and I opened my eyes. She smiled at me, and her lips parted into a beautiful fanged smile. "What's this?" she whispered and laughed softly like an eastern wind. "An intruder—with eyes of blue."

No anger in her voice or in her eyes.

I wanted to explain why I had entered her home but couldn't find the words, and my vanity wouldn't allow me to admit that I was foolish enough to believe she was human.

"It's all right," she said. "My name is Elenore Cohen."

I was silent, and she brushed the strands of my shaggy black hair from my eyes.

"Your name?"

"Adam," I stuttered. "My name is Adam Gold."

"A beautiful name for a beautiful face," she answered.

"I'm sorry," I said. "I shouldn't have come here." I turned, prepared to leave, but she stopped me.

I was supposed to take a wicked mortal and return to Relone.

"I must leave," I said.

"Wait."

I turned back to face her. It was like my body froze—like I was unable to turn away from her.

"You haven't fed," she whispered.

"No."

"Neither have I."

I furrowed my brow, trying to figure out what she was going to say.

"Come with me."

"With you?" I asked. "With you where?"

"Out there," she said with a laugh, pointing toward the window. "The city awaits."

I couldn't feed with her. I was to return to Relone. I had to say no. I opened my mouth to argue, but something else entirely happened. "The city does," I said. "Let us go."

Her smile broadened. I tried asking myself why I would not say no to her, why she had such power over me. It didn't seem to matter. Her beauty was mesmerizing.

We walked through the city, looking for the perfect victim.

"Only the wicked," I said to her. "I do not feed on innocent blood."

"Were you not planning to feed on me?" she asked with a hint of humor in her words.

"A moment of weakness," I said. "I'm new at this."

She nodded. "Very well. I know just the place."

We headed toward the dance hall, looking into the minds of the beautifully clad mortals. A man was to be our first victim. His mind was dark and a catalogue of murder and vicious attacks. Bloody and bruised bodies filled his memory, and he relished in them.

Elenore stood beside me while I drank my fill, waiting her turn to drain him.

"His blood tastes different somehow," she said.

"Is it not good?"

"It is better than good. It's—amazing."

"Evil blood," I answered. "Sometimes the taste is stronger."

She smiled at me, revealing her blood-stained teeth. "Another. I want another."

We fed on two more that night until the sun began peeking over the horizon and it was time to rest.

I returned to the crypt to find Relone already asleep, with a candle still burning. I snuffed out the flame and crawled into bed.

The next evening was the same and many more after that. I spent many nights with Elenore when I was supposed to be out hunting alone. Relone could not know. The jealousy would be unbearable for him.

"You are special," she said, dropping the dead human to the ground.

"What do you mean?"

"You're different, Adam. In many ways. You do not feed on innocent blood, and you have a house."

"You have a house."

"I am different too. I choose to live like a mortal, but it wasn't always so."

"No?"

She shook her head.

"My father was a rabbi in the Jewish temple. I never believed much about God, but of course, I could not confess that to him. I wanted to be good like I was taught, but once the dark blood was given to me, I felt a kind of darkness inside of me."

"I know that darkness," I said softly.

"I didn't resent it. In fact, I felt free. I had quite of list of mortal enemies. I brought them down without a second thought."

"You killed them?"

She took my hand and led me out of the alley, back to the street.

"I am not proud of it," she said, keeping her eyes forward. "It was something I did long ago—something I can never take back. Haven't you done things you wish you could take back?"

I thought of Mary and Madeline, and my chest burned with grief. "I have regrets. Many of them."

"I believe that's what it's like for our kind. Regret is part of the life."

"Yes."

"Come to my home with me," she said.

I was taken aback for a moment, not anticipating the sudden shift in conversation.

"I have blood there. The night is cold, and the streets are empty."

"You keep blood at your home?"

"Don't you?"

I shook my head.

"We do not always need to drink live. We can easily store the blood. It ages like a good wine, only getting better as time passes. What do you think?"

"I think there is too much I still don't know about being an immortal."

"Come," she said. "I'll show you."

We walked the empty streets to Elenore's English-style townhouse. She was a lover of the light, and hundreds of marvelous books were packed upon shelves. She switched on the lamp beside the couch in the front room of her house. The room lit up, and I could see all the valuable pieces of furniture and the colors in the rugs. It was beautiful.

"Wait here," she said. "I'll get you something to drink."

I watched the graceful way she moved as she left the room. She was a beauty who eased my loneliness—a shadow of long-lost love.

"Why do you feel pain?" she asked, sitting beside me, handing me a crystal wine glass filled with blood.

"What do you mean?"

"Why is it that even when you kill the evil, you feel pain?"

"It is my curse," I answered. "This life is a curse."

"Oh no, not at all. This life is a gift."

"You sound like Victor."

"Victor? Was he your maker?"

I nodded.

"Sounds like a wise man."

I heard the humor in her words, but irritation rocked through me.

"I'm sorry," she said. "I just mean that maybe you should not feel so guilty. You cannot change what you are."

I took a sip from my glass, tasting the robust, rich taste unlike any I tasted before. "This is incredible."

She pulled her dark hair over her shoulder and rested her head against the loveseat. "Like an aged wine."

"Yes."

She smiled kindly at me and moved a bit closer, sharing the warmth from the blood.

Chapter Ten

ELENORE GAZED at the boy on the ground. She ruffled through his clothes, finding his money. She kissed his forehead.

"You were lovely," she whispered. "It is a shame this must be your fate."

I looked at her with obvious shock in my expression.

"What is it?"

"You're just so…cavalier about it all."

"He was lovely," she said. "But he was also evil— wicked to his deepest foundation. This is what he deserved. There is no evil in that."

I sighed, continuing down the streets. We stalked a married couple.

A tall man with black hair like my own, he was rich and elegant. The woman that stood beside him was lovely as well. She had fiery red hair and eyes of green like the sea after a wicked storm. It was a strange thing—both people were desperately in love but planning murders of each other. They were walking arm in arm innocently on their way to an evening ball.

"How lovely," I heard Elenore say under her breath. "A murder of the loved ones. Classic."

"God," I mumbled. "Trahison."

"Betrayal?" She chuckled. "Yes."

"It disgusts me."

"It makes me happy in a strange way," she whispered. "We get to choose their fate."

"Do we?"

"In a way. They can die one of three ways."

"What do you mean?"

She laughed. "Well—swiftly, slowly, or simply become one of us."

"No!" I cried. "I would rather watch one suffer than become like us."

"Why do you find so much evil in the creation?" she asked. "It's a beautiful thing. It's miraculous—that we can create our own creatures, be as God."

"Be as God," I mumbled. "Be as the devil."

She smiled. "I'll take the man."

"I guess that leaves miss lovely for me."

We quickened our movement, and in a dark alleyway, we took them silently and swiftly. I wept as I often do.

Elenore stroked my hair. "What's hurting you, Adam?"

I shook my head. "It's nothing."

"Do not tell me you are grieving the death of our victims."

"I am not like you, Elenore. I do grieve. It is what I do. It is who I am."

She stared at me then leaned in and kissed my forehead. "You are lovely. So lovely."

We returned to her home again that night to relish in the feeling of being human. I followed her to the sitting room.

She stared at me and brushed my hair away from my eyes. I saw the way she looked at me—the way she smiled.

"There is something about you," she said, "something that makes me want you near me always."

"Can you be certain?" I asked, moving closer to her. "Certain that you feel this way?"

She nodded calmly, almost in a shy manner. "I truly adore you," she said, pressing her cheek against my chest.

I felt so weak when I was around her. I had so little self-control. I was not the powerful being I felt I was supposed to be. I embraced her, stroking her soft hair. I glanced in the mirror on the wall behind her and smiled. As I thought—it was Adam Gold. It was the vampire with the sweet eyes of blue.

"The daytime sky is within your eyes," she whispered. She stared into me as if she were trying to find daylight within me, as if she yearned for the light of the sun.

"Aw, my dark princess—black is our color. The night sky is within *your* eyes," I whispered back. She looked so unhappy, but when I spoke of her beauty and told her that her eyes held our world, she smiled.

I kissed her softly; her lips were warm. I lowered her upon the couch so I could lie above her. I realized she felt so much smaller as she lay beneath me, more delicate than a young mortal child. How could I touch her with my strength?

A breath escaped her lips, almost as though she were incapable of speaking. I backed away from her suddenly.

"Adam...?" she whispered.

My heart began pounding in my chest. A chill passed through me. I let that icy torture embrace me. She sat up, and I could tell she was having trouble keeping from crying.

"Adam?" she whispered again.

"Elenore, please—" My voice was cut off. Was I crying? "I can't tell you."

Then the tears came. I couldn't look at her when she was weeping. It was torture.

"What did I do?" she asked.

"You made me care," I replied. "Do not make me say it—please! It will result in pain—so much pain!"

How could I care for her? Why must I fall weak against her skin? She was far too beautiful, far too strong for me to be able to deny my feelings for her. But what about Mary and Rayne?

I knew I should leave; I needed to get out of there before I made a terrible mistake.

She knew these thoughts, and trying to make me stay, she whispered, "I love you."

I came back from my mind. "No, Elenore," I whispered, trying desperately to hold in my tears. Chills and tremors grew in my chest. "No!" I said again. "Do not say it!"

"I love you!" she said again, this time stronger —louder!

I covered my ears. She was yelling now, those three

wicked words, over and over until I thought my own cries would destroy me.

I let out a scream—no words, only an ear-piercing cry. The mirrors in the room shattered, and I could hear my Elenore's high-pitched yells as she jumped away from the scattered glass.

"Stop!" she cried. "Adam, stop!"

Her ears were covered with her hands until she lay covering her head with her arms. I realized my own screams were drawing blood from our ears as the windows cracked.

"You can shatter all the glass in the city!" she yelled.

Then let me shatter it! Let me scream!

Her words were slowly beginning to fade from my mind. My screams quieted. I was growing tired. My voice sank down to whimpers, and I fell out cold upon the floor.

"Fool," Relone scolded. "How could you!"

"I am not ashamed!" I yelled back.

"Simply because you are beautiful, Adam, simply because you know I can't refuse you, does not mean you are invincible. It does not mean you can do anything. Don't you understand? Love her and you finish us both!"

I only stared at him.

"You're so good," he whispered. "So good."

I could feel his breath on my neck, his cold lips upon my cheek. "You are my child now." He stroked my black hair and moved the strands away from my beautiful eyes. "You think you can do anything, don't you, Adam?"

"Relone, I cannot live alone! I cannot live without her. I need her as my nightly companion!"

A glimmer of anger danced across his eyes. It frightened me but left so quickly it appeared as if it was never actually there.

"Alone?" he asked, stepping closer. "You have me, Adam. Do you know who loves her? Who else?"

"What are you talking about?"

"There is another. Another more powerful than us both."

"Another vampire?"

"Verarsoe," he said. "Commonly known as The King. The time will come when she must go to him. If The King finds out about your affections, he will destroy you both!"

"I do not fear The King," I said.

"You should. You do not know him like I do, Adam. He is the king for a reason. He is more powerful than anyone."

"What can I do? Just leave her? Relone, I care for her."

"There's more," he started. "The King is the keeper of the most sacred of things."

"And what is that?"

"It's often called The Book of Shadows. It is the bible of darkness. He is not only all powerful, he knows of things no one else does." He stepped in front of me, forcing me to look into his terrified eyes. "He has more power than you could ever imagine. The oldest any of us will probably ever meet!"

"Is he…evil?"

"I'm not sure," he answered. "He may say he is, but I think there is a lot of goodness inside him that he would deny."

"Why does he want my Elenore?"

"He chose her," he answered. "Elenore's father was immortal as well, which I am sure she failed to mention."

I couldn't hide the shock on my face.

"He was a member of Verarsoe's coven, a terrible coven that worshiped him. Verarsoe had given him the dark gift in exchange for his daughter. He swore his daughter to The King long ago. Years later, he grew to hate The King, and he fled the coven, taking Elenore with him."

"Verarsoe let him run?"

"I'm not finished yet," he continued. "There was a price to pay for this sin. Her father—Michael Cohen—was destroyed. Burned by Verarsoe himself. The time is coming when Elenore must fulfill her father's payment."

"Why didn't you tell me any of this before now?" I yelled. "You knew about her and me before now, didn't you?"

He didn't reply.

"Didn't you?"

"I had hoped it wouldn't grow to anything more than a friendship," he said. "I'm sorry. I didn't realize that you would care for her the way you do."

"No," I whispered sadly. "*I'm* sorry. I knew it would result in pain, and I did nothing to stop it. *I'm* sorry."

"You did what you could," he said, kissing my forehead. "You did what you could. It is not your fault that she loves you."

It rained the next night, and I walked alone, hunting the streets for food. I took a lovely murderess that night, the woman with the yellow hair, who murdered her brother's wife; her blood was sweet with evil. I contemplated whether or not I should return to the Cohen house. Was she waiting for me? Perhaps...but what would Relone do if he found out I had gone to see her again?

I returned, feeling a bit embarrassed from the reaction the previous time, but she seemed to not even remember. She smiled as soon as she saw me before she could stop herself. Her beauty captivated me the way it usually did. I hugged her to me.

Once again, she had confessed her love for me, and once again, I shunned her, but I refrained from screaming as I had done before.

"Please, don't shut me out," she pleaded.

I turned away from her; I felt weak whenever I looked into her eyes.

"Adam?" she whispered. "My beauty with the daylight eyes."

I turned to see that she was crying but smiling

through her tears as she spoke the words of my charm. I had done it. I had looked into her eyes, and I knew that I could hold it back no longer, and I regretted it before I even said it.

"Aw, Elenore," I whispered. "My dark princess with the eyes of night—you are so dear to me."

I kissed her cheeks, tasting the sweet liquid, savoring its pleasure.

"Are you certain?" she questioned in a whisper.

"I am."

Deep inside me was this discomfort, this nervous worry. Now she had me at my most vulnerable state. I had confessed I cared for her, confessed that she was dear to me, and though I was not in love with her, my feelings were enough for her to cling to. There was no going back.

"I'm not afraid," she whispered.

"Neither am I," I answered although I was terrified.

We lay close, wrapped in each other's arms and soon falling fast asleep.

When I awoke, she was still near me, dreaming peacefully.

Colors splashed the eastern skies but not enough to harm me. I left her house, racing back to the catacomb. I walked down the stone steps quietly, being sure not to wake Relone if he had been sleeping, but when I saw him, he was sitting on a coffin, staring at the floor.

"All night?" I heard him say without looking up at me. "All day?"

I sighed and looked at him without responding.

"Adam," he started. "How? Why?"

I sighed. "She's—it's like she has a sort of power over me. I'm so weak when I'm around her."

"You left me here all day—alone."

"Relone, I'm sorry."

"You don't need Elenore—you need me."

"You know I could never leave you, Relone. Life without you? I couldn't even imagine!"

"Do I have to tell you again?" he snapped. "About The King and his love for her?"

I shook my head. "No. No, Relone, you do not."

Chapter Eleven

"YOU MUST PROTECT ME," she wept, clinging to my ankles. "Please, don't let him take me away from you."

"Elenore, it's not that easy," I said. "How can we deny someone with his power?"

"I don't want to go to him. I want to stay with you."

"I know," I whispered. "That isn't enough."

I cradled her against my chest as sobs tore from her. She jolted away from me in an instant with her eyes wide and alert.

"What is it?" I asked.

"Do you smell that?"

My mouth fell open. I would know that scent anywhere. It was the scent of destruction.

"Fire," she whispered, then screamed, "Fire!"

I sprang the window, prying it open only to be thrust backward by a burst of flames. The fire spread, enveloping the room. The heat was intense, burning my insides even though I did not breathe. The smoke was thick, obstructing my view. I tried calling out for Elenore, but my throat was scorched.

I sank to my knees, forcing my eyes to stay open. I lay on the floor as the flames threatened to swallow me, but I refused to lose consciousness.

Where were they now? The angels with their silken wings to drag me down to hell? Where was the light at the end of the tunnel? The open door, the judgment?

As I lay prepared for death, an unfamiliar face appeared before me. Long, black hair and black eyes. A flawless, ageless face quavering with devastation like water behind the flames. I knew by his eyes—their age. It was him. It was The King.

I reached out to him, or I tried to, but in an instant, he was gone. My eyes fluttered closed, and even as I tried to stay awake, I felt myself slipping out of consciousness.

I felt my tired body being lifted from the floor. The hands that held me felt strong and firm. I let myself fall against his body as we rose through the smoke, captivated by his strength as I always was.

He laid me gently upon the cobblestone outside the house. After a fit of coughs, I looked around, searching for Elenore. I sat up, turning, but I didn't see her.

"Where's Elenore?"

"Oh, I'm sorry, Adam. It's too late for her."

"No! Relone, where is she?"

"It's too late for her," he repeated.

"No, we must go back." I stood to my feet, feeling pain spread through my limbs. I stumbled forward, but Relone pulled me back.

"Adam, no. You can't go back in there."

I screamed, struggling in his grasp, watching the fire engulf Elenore's home, spreading like a flood.

"I'm sorry," Relone said. "I couldn't have saved her if I tried. She's gone."

And I wept.

Now, of course, I could not let him get away with this. Verarsoe had murdered my Elenore, with the intention of destroying me.

My grief pained Relone, but it wasn't enough to sway him.

"He is too strong, Adam," he said. "There is nothing that can be done."

"He knows I live," I said. "Relone, he will come after me. It's not over."

He sighed. "Verarsoe will not harm you."

"And why not?" I demanded. "Why wouldn't he kill me?"

"Because losing you would destroy me."

"And why does that matter?"

"Because Verarsoe would not wish to cause me pain, Adam. Because he loves me."

About the Author

Sara J Bernhardt is an author and poet who has been writing since a very young age and is a winner of several poetry and short story contests. It is clear that Bernhardt writes in a realistic tone while still creating the enthralling feeling of fantasy. Her writing puts readers in a world that they will truly love to be a part of. Though the writing is edgy and catching it is also not too complex which makes it a comfortable and enjoyable read for everyone.

You can follow Sara at these locations:

Facebook:
www.facebook.com/Sara-J-Bernhardt
Amazon:
www.amazon.com/Sara-J.-Bernhardt
Website
www.sjbernhardt.com

Other Works by Sara J. Bernhardt

https://www.amazon.com/Sara-J.-
Bernhardt/e/B07DNFCH5J/

Summer's Deceit (Hunters Trilogy – Book 1): Jane
Callahan is a reclusive, seventeen-year-old high school
student dealing with the death of her beloved brother. Her
home in Southern California with her mother is a constant
reminder of her loss and pain. In hopes of escaping her
past she moves to North Bend Oregon to live with her
father, where she meets a beautiful boy named Aidan
Summers. Jane is intrigued by his looks as well as his
unusual ways of attempting to get her attention. After
months of uncommon conversation and frustration, an
uncertain romance brews between Jane and Aidan, but
Aidan has a ghastly secret that could destroy everything.

Summer's Shadow (Hunters Trilogy – Book 2): Aidan
Summers, a seventeen-year-old, stunningly beautiful
genius, somehow finds his way into the life of Jane

Callahan; a lovely girl trapped in soggy North Bend, Oregon. In this new Tale by Sara J. Bernhardt, Aidan relates his side of the story. All of his dark secrets are revealed and all of his motivations behind his strange ways become known as the story unravels in a captivating narrative of suspense, romance, courage...and murder.

Summer's Redemption (Hunters Trilogy – Book 3): The secret alliance of The Silver Wing and the waging war with their evil rival, The Sevren, come into full view in a new light. The evil that still lurks and stirs behind the supposed destruction of The Sevren steps out of the shadows and spins a new tale of adventure, suspense, romance, mystery and terror.

Taboo love stories give you a special thrill?
Rebecca Stewart had never let things get personal with
her students; a mistake that could cost her far more than a
broken heart.

Jason and his friends enjoyed tormenting teachers. When
they set their sights on Miss Stewart, nothing would
prevent them from bringing her down.

Avoiding Jason's advances and navigating an epic clash
of wills, the young woman felt relieved to see graduation
day finally arrive. Little did she know, it wouldn't end
there. Pregnant and alone, she could only keep her secrets
for so long.

After one of the boys is found murdered, the police haul
her in, but she denies having done anything wrong. Can
she convince them of the truth before all three of the
young men fall victim to a killer, forcing her to raise her
child alone?

Made in the USA
Columbia, SC
12 June 2021

39970862R00070